# Love and Reruns in Adams County

**Also by Mark Spencer**

*Spying on Lovers*

# Love and Reruns
# in Adams County

A NOVEL

## Mark Spencer

Fawcett Columbine
New York

All rights reserved under International and Pan-American Copyright
Conventions. Published in the United States by Ballantine Books,
a division of Random House, Inc., New York, and simultaneously in Canada
by Random House of Canada Limited, Toronto. The first half of this work previously
appeared in a volume entitled *Wedlock* published by Walermark Press in 1989. Some
brief passages appeared in different form in short stories published in *Gambit
Magazine*, *Beloit Fiction Journal*, and *The Laurel Review.*

Library of Congress Cataloging-in-Publication Data:
Spencer, Mark, 1956-
Love and reruns in Adams County / Mark Spencer. — 1st ed.
p.  cm.
ISBN 0-449-90899-2
1.  Poor—United States—Fiction.  I. Title.
PS3569.P4536L68  1993
813'.54—dc20                                        93-22126
                                                        CIP

Text design by Beth Tondreau Design

Manufactured in the United States of America
First Edition: February 1994
10  9  8  7  6  5  4  3  2  1

For Krista, David, and Evelyn Spencer
and for
Corina

It ought to make us feel ashamed when we talk like we know what we're talking about when we talk about love.

—*Raymond Carver*

# PART I

# 1985

# One

One spring morning when Pamela is feeling optimistic about having a good day (after all, good things are bound to happen *some*time), her mother phones to tell her Lon's father has died.

"It was in the paper yesterday, but I knew you were workin', and I didn't want to bother you last night."

Pamela divorced Lon nearly six years ago. "So what about it?"

There's silence and a little static. Then her mother says, "I thought you'd want to know. I thought you liked Lon's dad."

Pamela doesn't say anything for a moment. Now she feels guilty, and her day is ruined for sure. "Yeah, I liked him. It's just it's been years since I saw him."

"He was a good man—Lon's dad."

"I know."

"He had a hard time after his wife passed away."

"Mom, I gotta get ready for work."

"Okay. I'm sorry I took up your time. I just thought you'd want to know since you-know-who will be coming back from wherever he is. His dad didn't have anybody else to leave that farm to."

"I didn't hear you, Mom, 'cause I don't want to know or think about it."

"I hear that farm got real run-down."

"Okay. 'Bye."

"You still havin' that weird dream about you and Lon?"

"No. 'Bye." Pamela hangs up.

A couple of years ago Pamela told her mother about the dream she keeps having—that she's been having ever since about a year after she divorced Lon. She needed to tell somebody, but telling Mom was a mistake because Mom keeps reminding her about it just when Pamela's managed to put it out of her head.

She goes into the bathroom and starts putting on makeup, getting ready to go to work at the McDonald's in Peebles. She thinks about putting on eye liner, but her hand won't stop shaking. Then she wonders why she bothers anyway. She grabs a hunk of her hair and pulls it around to her nose and is certain she smells McDonald's grease.

Restaurant work is all she figures she can do. The mobile-home park she lives in is just outside of West Union, but West Union doesn't have a McDonald's, just Jack's Eats. Jack and his wife, Louise, run the place by themselves. Pamela wouldn't want to work there anyway. The last time she ate there, she got a piece of bread half covered with mold.

Bobby, her second husband, is in the spare bedroom of

their trailer, fooling with his toys. She has no idea what he does in there with them. He hasn't had a job for a year and a half, but he tells people he's a dealer in rare, collectible toys. For a few months after he got laid off from the feed mill, he applied for a job every once in a while, but nothing ever came through. He spent most of his time watching TV. Around eleven every night he'd make a run to the Taco Bell in Peebles because, he said, he had a craving for burritos. This was his routine.

Now he spends a lot of his time driving all over southern Ohio and northern Kentucky, buying toys at garage sales and flea markets. He has dozens of rusty, beat-up wagons, trucks, cars, tricycles, airplanes, and spaceships.

At first Pamela didn't believe people actually collected old toys and spent a lot of money on them. Then she remembered her aunt, who had hundreds of little spoons with state slogans and seals on them and the names of tourist attractions like Yellowstone Park, the Everglades, and Disney World (that one had a handle shaped like Mickey Mouse). Her aunt ordered the spoons from a catalog. And there was Pamela's sixty-year-old cousin, who collected baseball cards. He had a Hank Aaron rookie card he claimed he paid a hundred dollars for—a picture on a piece of cardboard. People collected *anything.* Bobby told her he knew a guy who owned over three thousand beer cans.

Every other day or so Bobby tells Pamela he figures he has around ten thousand dollars' worth of toys that he's spent only four hundred dollars on.

But so far he hasn't sold anything. Once he took several toys to Cincinnati to see whether a dealer there wanted to buy some of them, but Bobby brought everything home. Pamela didn't ask what happened, and he didn't say. For a week he didn't go to any flea markets or garage sales, just watched game shows and cartoons on TV and read *True Crime* magazines. Then one afternoon he went out and came back with a rusty tricycle that had a great big front wheel and said, "God Jesus, Pam, can you believe I paid only forty dollars for this? This thing's worth ten times that much. Got it from an old woman that's movin' to an old-folks home. She didn't know nothin'."

Pamela was mixing pancake batter for supper and trying to figure out in her head how many hours she had to work at McDonald's to make forty dollars.

On her way to work in her '74 Maverick, Pamela can't help thinking about the dream. She and Lon are making love, and at first Lon has his torso arched above her, and he's tanned and muscular and beautiful with his teeth and eyes flashing. Then he lowers himself and kisses her shoulder and neck, and she smooths his soft hair and looks at the ceiling, which starts out white, turns pink, and finally becomes red. When he raises himself up, he's fat and pale, and his features are horribly distorted, as if he's in terrible pain.

She realizes just today that he looks a lot like the Nazis in *Raiders of the Lost Ark*, who get their faces melted off by the wrath of God. He looks the way the Nazis do when their faces first start melting.

# Two

The summer Pete Rose will break Ty Cobb's record for most career hits by a major-league baseball player, Lon Peterson returns home.

He's been gone six years. Now his daddy has died and left him the family farm. When he reaches Adams County in the hills of southcentral Ohio, Lon first drives to the county seat, West Union, to see his daddy's lawyer. As he enters the town, he reads the sign saying the population is 3,658. The town is shrinking. Pete Rose has more hits than West Union has people. The front windows of William's Hardware, Ed's Diner, and Be Beautiful Beauty Salon are empty and cloudy with dirt; they're all shut down.

Main Street is full of potholes. Farmers are committing suicide. But Lon's daddy just died of a wrecked heart. On the phone long-distance the lawyer said Daddy fell over in the kitchen.

The lawyer's office is near the courthouse, next to Jack's Eats. The lawyer gets up from behind his desk, steps around it, and shakes Lon's hand. He's fragile-looking in an old gray suit. He smiles, his teeth small and yellow. Then he frowns and tells Lon he's terribly sorry about his daddy.

Lon remembers meeting him eight or nine years ago. Lon, who was fifteen or sixteen, and his daddy were coming out of the barbershop, and the lawyer was going in. They all stopped on the sidewalk, and Lon's daddy and the lawyer talked for a minute. Lon didn't listen. He saw a woman in a tight black dress walking up the steps of the courthouse across the street, her back to him. She had shiny blond hair and smooth, slim legs. He tried to imagine her naked. Then at the top of the steps she turned around, as if she had heard someone call her name and looked down at Lon, who couldn't help making a sour face—she was wall-eyed and her face flamed with acne. She quickly turned away.

The lawyer hands Lon some papers and says, "Have you been away from home long?"

Lon looks up from the papers. The lawyer's desk is made of dark, heavy wood, and the walls are covered with walnut paneling; there are dark bookcases and dark books. Lon feels like saying, *You mean you don't know?* Instead he says, "You know any real-estate agents?"

After he's finished with the lawyer, Lon drives a round-about route to the farm so that he can go past the mobile-home park. He slows down and takes a look. A collection of rusty cracker boxes on concrete blocks, swarms of dirty little kids, homely women hanging up wash. He speeds up.

The road the farm is on has never been paved, is still

gravel. The neighbors and their place look unchanged. They have nine acres on the side of a rocky hill and live on their tobacco patch and county welfare. Most of the paint has peeled off their little house. Five rusty car corpses sit in the front yard. On the porch, in straight-back wooden chairs, two obese women in sleeveless dresses sit with their hands on their thighs, their tanned upper arms looking like hams. Standing by the chair of one of the fat women is a pregnant girl about seventeen. As Lon drives by, she brushes her lank hair out of her face with her hand and tucks it behind an ear and yells something at a little boy playing on the hood of one of the old cars. The child is naked except for a T-shirt with Pete Rose's face on it. Lon waves, and they all stare back.

The farm that now belongs to Lon has eighty acres. Each year his daddy planted soybeans, alfalfa, corn, and a patch of tobacco. The house needs paint, and some of the shingles from the roof are lying in the yard, but the house looks better than the tall, narrow barn, which leans way to the east and won't be standing much longer, he figures.

When he was a kid, Lon would spend hours throwing a baseball against the side of the barn and catching it on the rebound instead of doing his chores. He kept track of how many times he caught rebounds and how many times he missed. His daddy never painted the section of the barn where Lon's baseball wore or knocked the paint off.

The barn is huge, and when it falls, there should be quite a crash.

Lon never liked life on this farm much, mainly because of the work, but looking around at all the weeds and peeling paint and rusty barbed wire, he feels sad. All this couldn't have happened in the six weeks it took the lawyer to locate him in Oregon, where he was selling encyclopedias door-to-door.

He realizes that this deterioration probably started the summer he left home to play minor-league baseball. The same summer his mama died of a stroke. His wife, Pamela, came home for the funeral, but no one could persuade Lon to come. He was afraid of the crying people and his mama's dead body and was ashamed of what was happening to his baseball career.

Now he wishes he'd paid his last respects to Mama. The day of the funeral he played in a game in Macon, Georgia, and struck out four times.

He remembers his daddy constantly sneaking up on his mama (while she washed dishes or threw feed to the chickens—anytime) and grabbing her from behind, grabbing her big breasts and saying, "I just *love* milk melons."

She'd push him away and point at Lon, who would be grinning. "The boy, Frank. The boy," she'd say, her face flushed the color of a rooster's comb.

When she died, Daddy must have been broken up bad, worse than he let on in his short letters scrawled in pencil. The place shows how bad.

Lon never saw him again after he left home to play for the Raleigh, North Carolina, Rebels. After Raleigh released him and Pamela divorced him, Lon and his daddy exchanged only a few letters and talked on the phone once a year at Christmas, Lon calling from wherever he happened to be, an ocean of static filling up long gaps in their conversation.

Before he goes inside the house, Lon walks out behind the barn and looks off at the woods and thinks of growing marijuana. A lot of guys in the minors smoked it (only major-leaguers could afford cocaine). When he walks back toward the house, he looks at his car, a '72 Pinto, half rust and half orange. It has bald tires and a cracked windshield.

He unlocks the back door and enters the kitchen. On the

table there are stale crackers and an open jar of peanut butter and ants. In the refrigerator are three eggs, sour milk, and an empty ketchup bottle.

In the living room there are cracker crumbs on the sofa. The flowery wallpaper he remembers his mama hanging when he was still playing with toy soldiers is faded. He sees his mama sitting on his daddy's lap on the sofa. *You're a devil, Frank.*

Everything is covered with dust. The whole house smells like puke.

*Let me up, Frank. There's the boy. The boy. Hi, sugar.*

Six years ago Lon stood in this living room with suitcases at his feet, his daddy hugging Pamela, his mama touching Lon's face, tears in her eyes. He was happy as hell to get out.

He turns on the old black-and-white TV. The picture is snowy but good enough. He has watched a lot of TV in the last six years and sits down on the sofa to watch a game show he's familiar with. Then he remembers the beer he bought before crossing the county line—Adams County is dry. When he goes out to the car to get it, he feels a little bit of a chill. Wispy clouds have blocked the sun, although most of the sky is bright blue. There are no sounds except the breeze in the tall grass and weeds and trees. The lawyer sold all the animals.

Lon opens all the doors and windows to air the house out. He drinks beers in front of the TV. He drinks one can after another. When it gets dark, the sounds of crickets come through the open windows and doors. Then the sounds of things moving in the weeds. Lon gets off the sofa and shuts the house up, then goes back to the TV and drinks more beer. He figures he'll keep drinking until he feels ready.

# Three

Lately Pamela has been having the dream almost every night. She's scared of seeing Lon again but isn't sure why. It's been nearly six years since she laid eyes on him. And last she heard anything about him, rumor was that he was in South Dakota. She's not sure she can accurately remember what he looks like, although she knows he's neither the beautiful man nor the horrible man of her dream. She has thrown away every picture she had of him, but she has half a photograph that shows her in her high school prom dress with a disembodied arm around her shoulder, Lon's throwing arm—he was a catcher and proud of how he could pick off base runners.

She cries some mornings, remembering the dream, while she makes breakfast and Bobby is still asleep or in the bathroom. She has always liked having the radio on mornings because the music gets her going, but she has to turn it off now if a song from six or seven years ago comes on.

The worst thing to happen recently was seeing a movie on TV that she saw at her parents' house with Lon one New Year's Eve. Her parents weren't home, and she and Lon were watching a Marx brothers movie because Lon thought they were really funny. Eventually, without a word and still half watching the movie, Lon started undressing her. She knew he would, but it took him longer to get around to it than she expected. While they made love on the carpet, she couldn't help glancing at the TV, the only light in the room.

She can't forget Groucho wiggling his eyebrows while Lon was on her. There was a close-up on Harpo's dopey, silent laugh at the exact moment Lon came. A public-service announcement for libraries appeared as he rolled off her.

One morning last week, after "Donahue," Pamela was changing channels, and that Marx brothers movie was on. She sat on the floor close to the TV. After the close-up on Harpo's silent laugh, she expected a commercial, but the movie kept going. She flicked off the set and stared at her reflection in the dark screen.

Pete Rose is one reason she thinks she's having the dream more often. He is back with the Cincinnati Reds as player-manager after being gone five years, and there's a lot of hoopla about his breaking Ty Cobb's record. There's news about him every day—whether he got a hit in the most recent game.

Pete Rose was Lon's hero.

In high school Lon was the greatest baseball player in the history of Adams County. Three days after Pamela and Lon graduated, they got married. Lon wore his only suit, a dark-green one, and his baseball spikes. He had polished them and wire-brushed the cleats. The minister wouldn't let him wear his baseball cap during the ceremony, but at the reception in the Methodist church's basement, Lon put it on. Bud Morris, the star pitcher of the West Union High School Indians, was best man and also wore spikes.

Pamela and Lon spent their wedding night at the Holiday Inn in Portsmouth. She found it strange to make love in that cool, dark room that had a smell reminding her of hospitals. People out in the hall walking past their door always seemed to be laughing. She was used to Lon's car (they made love at her parents' house only three times) or, when his parents were gone, his room, the walls covered with pictures of famous baseball players and the top of the dresser crowded with trophies, little gold men swinging baseball bats. She loved the smell of his bed.

It was strange to make love not looking at the rip in the convertible top of Lon's '64 Skylark or at Pete Rose's grinning gap-toothed face.

The next day they drove to Raleigh, North Carolina— almost. Lon's Skylark gave out fifty miles north of the city, and they ended up having to take a bus the rest of the way. Lon had always claimed his car was a classic and worth a pile of money, but he paid forty dollars to have it towed to a junkyard. Pamela found it hard to believe he could be so wrong about something.

There was a used-car dealer in Raleigh who sponsored a late-night movie, and as the summer wore on, Pamela paid closer and closer attention to the cars the dealer showed off. She sat on the threadbare sofa in her and Lon's furnished apartment near the ball park and watched movies like *Zombie Brides*, hosted by this car-hawking man in a vampire costume. Between segments of the movie the Vampire stood in a well-lighted car lot in front of used cars, his pale face and blood-red lips always smiling, and told´stupid jokes, read fan mail, and talked about cars: "We have late-night specials on all our quality preowned cars. Now, folks, despite the way I'm dressed, our prices will not suck the life out of you. Prices are low. Credit is easy. We're open all night. Our salesmen are ready to serve you. Come on down between midnight and four, and you can be on television." Sometimes while talking about a car, he would lay hands on it, his palms flat on the hood, as if blessing it or driving out all the gremlins. Every once in a while he held somebody's elbow and said, "Tell us your name."

"Edward Dixon."

"Ed just bought that seventy-one Monte Carlo I showed you earlier," the Vampire said to the camera. "He beat the rest of you folks to it, but come on down anyway. We're at the corner of May and Southwest Expressway. We have plenty of cars. Ed, you want to say hi to anybody?"

"My wife."

"Okay."

"Hi, Irene." He gave a little wave, his shoulders slightly hunched. He reminded Pamela of Gomer Pyle. A lot of people in North Carolina did.

"Okay. Thank you, Edmund Dixon." Pointing at Pamela, the Vampire said, "You, too, can be on TV. Just come on down and take a look at our cars."

One night, near the end of the summer and the baseball season, alone because Lon was on a road trip, Pamela felt a strong urge to go down to the Vampire's lot and buy a '70 Camaro he kept showing off. Its fire-engine-red paint job had been polished so that it shone in the television lights like a precious jewel.

She still thinks about that Camaro every once in a while, and when she does, she feels she missed an opportunity, missed taking a road that would have led to an entirely different life. California comes to her mind. A hot sun. But a cool breeze too.

It was only $750. She thought about the money in her and Lon's bank account, around $800, most of which her parents had given them. She had always liked Camaros, although she liked Trans Ams best. When the Skylark broke down, Lon told her that after he made it to the major leagues, he'd buy her a brand-new, fully loaded Trans Am.

By the middle of the summer, though, she knew she would never get it.

# Four

Lon never feels quite ready and passes out sometime during a rerun of "Love Boat." When he wakes up, Wile E. Coyote is falling off a cliff, and the Roadrunner is saying, "Beep beep."

He rubs his eyes and staggers to the kitchen, where rusty water comes out of the faucet, and he takes a long drink. Then he slides the plastic checkered curtains apart and looks at a field that's a mess of grass and weeds.

He remembers he dreamed about Pamela, although he can't recall the details of the dream. It was she he was trying to get ready for last night. Distance has always helped him not to think about her much, but since he started the drive across the country from Oregon, she's been on his mind constantly. Now that she is so close, he feels he has to see her. He hasn't the slightest idea what will happen when he sees her or what he will feel, but he can't help thinking that she's the only woman who can give him something he needs—some complex yet essential thing he can't put a label on. He has occasionally talked about Pamela to men he's gotten drunk with. Most of the drunks have said it's not healthy or normal to carry a torch for a woman so long. One old drunk told him to just remember that all pussy was pink. Lon recalls seeing this man vomit blood on a sidewalk in front of a mission. Six years ago Lon loved baseball and Pamela, and he lost them both.

He has heard that a lot of Vietnam vets have flashbacks and nightmares, and that's supposed to be why they can't live normal lives. Lon told a counselor at the junior college he attended one semester in California that he knew how those vets felt. They'd failed; he'd failed. The counselor smiled. Lon had gone to him because he never felt like studying. All he wanted to do was watch TV and sleep and get laid. The counselor said that baseball and Vietnam weren't at all alike. One was war, the other a game. Just a game. It wasn't really a very significant thing, a person would realize if he thought about it. The world could get along fine—in fact many people in the world did get along fine without baseball, he said, still smiling, his fingers twined together on top of his desk.

When Lon was in elementary school, he read biographies of the baseball greats—Babe Ruth, Lou Gehrig. The books said they were great men, beloved national heroes. He also read biographies of Abraham Lincoln and George Washington, and there was no difference between the presidents and the baseball players—the books all sounded the same.

In the seventies, when the Cincinnati Reds won six divisional titles, they were front-page news in Cincinnati. A winning streak of more than four games was cause for headlines: REDS WIN EIGHTH IN ROW. At the bottom of the page, below a picture of Pete Rose or Joe Morgan or Johnny Bench, below the picture's caption or pushed to page two, might be a headline like EARTHQUAKE KILLS THOUSANDS IN BOLIVIA.

Lon looked at the counselor, matched his smile, and said the world could get along without war, too, couldn't it?

While looking out the window over the kitchen sink, Lon notices his Pinto has a flat tire.

He searches the cabinets for breakfast foods, but all he finds is a bag of white beans and an unopened bottle of ketchup. His daddy loved white beans smothered in ketchup. Lon suddenly sees his daddy's heart pumping blood. Opening and closing like a fist. Then the image gets crazy—the heart looks old, sprouts gray hairs and warts. Lon goes into the living room and turns off the TV. In the silence he shivers.

He puts the spare tire on and kicks it. Then he kicks the Pinto's fender. He kicks the passenger door. The car rocks. He kicks the front bumper.

He backs away, his heart pounding, then turns toward the woods. "Marijuana," he says out loud. He walks toward the woods. Under the trees it's cool and dark. He looks as deep into the woods as he can and decides he won't grow marijuana. He thinks of jail. He's been there and didn't like it. He woke up in a small cell in Texas with dried blood and puke all down his shirt, one of the sleeves torn off. And when he remembers this, he remembers a nightclub called the Plucked Hen Inn, which used to be a chickenhouse, a hundred-and-fifty-foot cinder-block building with antique chicken-plucking machines in the corners and a nude dancer named Reba, who had a shaved pussy.

No, he's not going to grow marijuana, but he's also not going to be a goddamned farmer.

In the afternoon, in the middle of the Game of the Week (Saint Louis is playing in Chicago), the real estate agent Lon has been expecting drives up the long gravel driveway in a big Buick. The agent has bushy eyebrows and an olive complexion; his skin looks greasy. He has a white shirt on with the sleeves rolled up and a bright-green tie. His fingers are thick and short, and he grips Lon's hand a little too firmly.

While Lon shows him around, the agent keeps saying, "Okay, okay," and nodding his head thoughtfully.

"My daddy let the place get run-down."

"Well, he was old."

"He was sixty-one."

"You know, Lon, what would really make the value of this property shoot up?"

"I'm plannin' to do some work 'round the place."

"Besides that."

"What?"

"If somebody killed your neighbors and burned their house." He makes a squawking noise, and his belly jiggles.

Lon turns away so the guy can't see he's not even smiling and looks in the direction of the neighbors' place. They always had a swarm of kids, and he never knew all their names. The neighbors tended not to have much to do with anybody outside their family. But Lon remembers three grubby little kids, two boys and a girl, coming across the soybean field one day and up to the house to ask him for his autograph. No one had ever asked for his autograph before. Hell, he was only in high school. He went into his room and got three sheets of notebook paper and signed each one, making the letters of his name short and fat the way Pete Rose did.

The agent clears his throat and says it's a good idea to fix the place up. It can bring thirty-five thousand if they find some city people looking for a rural retreat and a tax break. Those kinds of buyers have been keeping the real estate business alive in this area, he says.

As he's about to leave, opening the door of the Buick, releasing new-car smell, the agent says, "By the way, I remember when you played ball at the high school."

Lon shrugs and grins, nods.

"You were the best damn player anybody'd ever seen around here. I remember that."

Lon looks up at the sun, squints, and says, "Thank you."

He drives recklessly on his way to Brown County to get beer. He feels good. A hundred feet past the county line he stops at Hilltop Store, a little place run by a bent, slow old woman, who has been selling beer to minors since World War II. Lon used to skid on the gravel lot up to the front door of the Hilltop in his Skylark, six or seven buddies—sometimes the whole starting lineup of the West Union High School baseball team—squeezed in the front and back seats. When he was sixteen, Lon would strut into the Hilltop, pick up a six-pack, and all the old woman ever said was, "Anything else, honey?"

The years have not changed her. Lon would swear she has always worn the same old loose long dress with a small flower print.

"How you doin' today, ma'am?" Lon says, setting three six-packs on the counter.

"Anything else, honey?"

"Nope."

She makes change from an old cigar box. Lon looks around, smells something he associates with old people's houses, but he doesn't know what it is. All the canned foods are covered with thin layers of dust. There's rust on some of the cans. Lon wonders what the expiration dates on them are. He thinks about how easy it would be to rob this woman.

Then without thinking about it, he says, "It's been a long time since I been in Ohio."

She counts out his change.

"But I grew up 'round here." He's not sure she's listening. "Ma'am?" She's looking into her cigar box. "Ma'am? Do you remember me?"

She puts the cigar box under the counter and turns aside, her left hand on her hip, her chin on her chest as if she's looking at her feet. Bald spots show through the wisps of her white hair. "Yes," she says.

"You do?"

"Yes."

Before he pulls onto the road, he opens a can. He's ecstatic. With thirty-five thousand dollars he can buy a new car and some nice clothes, and he's got an idea—a good idea for a change. He's going to become a real estate agent in Adams and Brown counties. A lot of local people will remember him from his high school playing days, and the city people from Cincinnati looking for rural retreats will take to him fast because everybody from Cincinnati is a baseball nut. In any case, people will definitely like him better than that dork trying to sell his daddy's farm.

Like the Reds, Lon was once front-page news—at least in Adams County in the *West Union Gazette* and the *Adams County Courier.* He hit .436 his senior year, was county Most

Valuable Player three years. Scouts from New York, Chicago, Cincinnati, Cleveland, and Pittsburgh came to see him play, sat in the rickety old bleachers and wrote in little notebooks, and shook his hand and put their arms around his manager's shoulders and ducked their heads, asking questions about him in low voices ("Is he disciplined?" "Has he had many injuries?"), and Mr. Daniels nodded emphatically and shook his head vigorously, wanting to see one of his boys make it to the big time.

Jesus, Lon thinks, if he could go back and freeze his life at that time, just be in high school for eternity. . . . For Christ's sake, he screwed three of the school's five cheerleaders.

He drives around, drinking, looking at houses and farmland. He could have a real estate office in West Union. It amazes him now that for all these years he was afraid to come home. What was he afraid of?

He feels higher than he's felt in a long time, and he heads out to the mobile-home park. He's ready.

# Five

Pamela has to park in a far corner of the McDonald's lot because the manager won't let any of "his girls" park near the "store." She thinks it's strange that Ray calls the place a "store" instead of a restaurant, and she's a little put off by the way he calls her and her co-workers "his girls." When she shuts off the engine, the Maverick shudders. The smells of Big Macs and french fries and exhaust fumes are in the air.

It's four in the afternoon, and they're getting ready for the supper-time rush. Pamela works mornings sometimes, evenings other times—whenever she's needed; sometimes she works double shifts.

Working the register is not too bad; it's a lot better than clearing off the tables of customers who don't bother to put their trash in garbage cans. Half-eaten Quarter Pounders with ketchup and mustard oozing out make her kind of sick. Occasionally somebody will chew up part of a hamburger, then spit it out on the tray. She wonders whether people sometimes do that out of meanness, the way Betty Jo Jenkins spits on the hamburgers and french fries when Ray's not around and says, "Just a little seasoning. We do it all for you." Betty Jo is a big, fat, trashy woman who recently lost her welfare because she had a man living with her and her five kids.

Mary Engler, a seventeen-year-old who attends the Church of Christ, is horrified by Betty Jo, but Carla, who brags all the time that she's going to get married instead of finishing high school, seems to just think Betty Jo's a greaseball.

"My fiancé showed me a cartoon in a dirty magazine," Carla says. Ray has just left. He frequently disappears for forty minutes or an hour; Carla and Betty Jo say they'd bet he's got a woman. "Well, in this cartoon it shows this girl in a McDonald's uniform down on her knees under a table doin' you-know-what with her . . . her mouth to some guy eatin' a Big Mac and smilin' real big." Carla demonstrates the smile. "Underneath the picture it said, 'We do it *all* for you.' Ain't that the funniest thing you ever heard?"

Betty Jo says, "Why don't you ask Ray if you can start doin' that?"

"Sometimes you're really disgusting, you know that?" Carla says.

"Nobody likes a tease, honey."

Pamela acts as if she's not listening. She doesn't have much to do with her co-workers. Except for Betty Jo and Ray, they're all in high school. None of them has a nickel's worth of knowledge about life.

Pamela laughs to herself when the girls fantasize out loud about getting married, but she never says anything. What's the point? She knows what it's like to be sixteen, seventeen, and to think all you need is a certain boy, a roof over your head, a TV, and a bed—paradise.

Mary Engler says she's proud to be a virgin and plans to stay that way until her wedding night.

Carla says, "Well, I'm willin' to do anything for Rick. We're gettin' married anyway."

"That doesn't make it right. What if he broke up with you? What if he got killed or something?"

Betty Jo says, "You ever have the opportunity to lose it, Mary?"

Mary turns red. Carla says, "I'll do anything to keep Rick. I'd kill myself if he ever broke up with me."

"That's a sin too."

"I love him."

"You should love Jesus more than anybody else."

Pamela suddenly remembers what Bobby looked like when he was a kid, skinny and pale, his hair long and lank. He grew up across the street from her, but she and Bobby never played together. Bobby never played with anybody. He was weird, and little girls didn't want to sit next to him or stand in line near him, including Pamela. When he was fourteen or fifteen, he still went trick-or-treating, walking the streets alone with a feed sack designed to hold a hundred pounds of shelled horse corn. He'd dress up like Snoopy or Adolf Hitler or Jesus Christ.

But he seemed sweet—and merely different—when Pamela came back home from North Carolina. At first, after the divorce, she dated Lon's friends, boys like Lon, jocks. When they'd come to her parents' house to pick her up, Bobby was often on his porch across the street. He sat on his porch year-round. In freezing weather he'd be sitting in the porch swing, smoking a cigarette. In summer he'd sit there without a shirt. His chest was pale and smooth, and Pamela always thought of a porcelain doll. When she went out on her dates, after the divorce, she'd give Bobby a little wave, mainly just because he was a neighbor. He'd nod and give her a shy smile.

On the dates the boys talked about themselves. Sometimes they asked about Lon, how he was doing, what he was doing. They asked her why Lon had such a bad season.

Then they grabbed her crotch and said, "Come on. You've been married."

Bobby took her to the Smoky Mountains for their honeymoon, a *real* honeymoon. Pamela considered it a good start. Each day of the trip Bobby gave her a gift first thing in the morning: a stuffed Smokey the Bear, a silver-plated necklace, a pair of gold-colored earrings, a bottle of Love's Baby Soft perfume, a music box that played "My Darling Clementine." He snuck off to buy the presents at gift shops near the motel while she napped or sunbathed or watched TV.

The sixth morning Bobby went through his usual routine: he sat on the edge of their bed, touched her shoulder, and said, "Wake up, baby. I got you a surprise."

Pamela sat up, cradling her Smokey the Bear, smiling. The slim straps on her nightgown had slipped off her shoulders. It took her eyes a moment to focus on the present Bobby held just inches from her face: a varnished outhouse about a foot high with JOHN sloppily painted across the door. "What is it?"

"Open the door." Bobby moved the outhouse even closer to her face.

When she opened the little door, thinking that maybe the real gift was inside, a grinning toothless plastic hillbilly with a disproportionately large penis squirted a thin stream of water on her.

Bobby fell off the bed and rolled on the floor like some fool on TV, maybe even a cartoon character, Pamela thought.

"That's disgusting." She wiped at her cheek and sniffed her hand. "That's just water, I hope."

"Hell no!"

"Ugh!"

"Yeah, it's only water." Bobby got up off the floor.

"It's still disgusting."

"I think it's funny as hell."

She and Bobby had drunk a lot of wine the night before, and now she was aware of her headache.

"It's stupid. That's what it is."

Bobby's face scrunched up so fast Pamela thought for a second she was dreaming. He glared and turned the color of raw steak. "Listen, woman, one of these days I might just be *gone.*"

# Six

The trailers are beat-up and old. Lon drives slow, looking at the names on the mailboxes. He vaguely remembers the guy Pamela's married to. The guy didn't play any sports. When Lon finds Pamela's trailer, he stays in his car, looking at it while he finishes a beer. The trailer is a two-tone aqua-and-white sixties model with an air conditioner sticking out a front window, chugging and dripping. He remembers a picture Pamela drew one time of the big house they were going to build after he made it to the major leagues and was making a million dollars a year.

It was going to be a brick house, she explained, because brick houses were safer in bad storms. The master bedroom would be huge with a round bed in the center of it. There would be a bedroom for each child, one boy and two girls, and the living room would have a big picture window; he and Pamela would look out at green mountains. The living room was to be painted gold.

# Seven

She comes home, and the screen door has a hole in it. It's hot outside, but the trailer is icy because Bobby has apparently let the window air conditioner run nonstop all day again. Pamela thinks of the electric bill.

Bobby's sitting in the dark. "Don't turn on the light," he says.

"Why not?"

"Just don't."

"I have to see, don't I?"

"Don't."

She flicks the switch. Bobby's T-shirt is torn. He's holding his gun in his lap. It's a little .22 pistol he bought not long ago.

"What's goin' on?" she says, scared.

"Nothin'."

A stack of *True Crime* magazines sits on the coffee table, which is chipped at every corner, the particleboard showing. Bobby started reading *True Crime* after he lost his job.

Pamela remembers that in high school a girl named Linda Sharp read *True Crime* in the lunch room. One day Linda told her about a woman who came out of her shower and found a man with a gun in her bedroom. He made her lie down on her bed naked, and he put the gun inside her and got her all worked up. Then he pulled the trigger.

Linda was smiling, and her eyes looked weird. The woman lived, she added after a minute. At the time Pamela thought Linda was just gross. Now she feels really sorry for her.

Pamela feels Bobby's eyes on her as she steps into the kitchenette and puts her purse on the counter.

"Lon was here," he says.

She feels light, as if she could float, but for a minute she can't even move her feet.

# Eight

It's morning, and Bobby is in the woods behind the mobile-home park, shooting holes in an old cake pan he leaned against an oak tree. He bought the gun a few weeks ago at a pawnshop after he donated a couple of his antique toys to the Brown County Hospital Children's Ward. He thought he deserved to give himself a present, so he bought the .22 pistol. He pretends the cake pan is the face of Pamela's ex-husband.

When he goes back to the trailer, Pamela is wearing her McDonald's uniform and washing the breakfast dishes. Bobby stands on the other side of the counter that separates the kitchen and the living room. He puts the pistol on the counter and looks at the pancake syrup on the plates Pamela's washing and thinks about how bad the pancakes were; she bought generic pancake mix again, although she knows he doesn't like it.

"Can't you steal us some Egg McMuffins?" he says. "I like Egg McMuffins and them sausage biscuits. Don't you get no fringe benefits, like all the Egg McMuffins your husband can eat?"

Pamela looks sideways at the gun and says, "You know I don't like that thing laying around."

"It ain't like we got kids that could get hold of it."

"Yeah, well, I just don't like it. I'm always afraid it's gonna get knocked on the floor and go off or something."

"There ain't nothin' to be afraid of." Bobby snatches up the pistol, puts the barrel to his temple, and pulls the trigger. Click.

Pamela staggers back from the sink with both hands on her heart. "One of these days you're gonna kill yourself."

When she takes them away from her chest, her wet hands leave a print on her blouse. Bobby aims at the print and pulls the trigger.

"What the hell's the matter with you?" Pamela yells.

"It ain't loaded, stupid."

"You're gonna shoot yourself or somebody else if you don't stop playing around."

"I guarantee you I'll shoot Lon if he ever comes around here again."

Pamela stares at the dirty dishwater and pulls the stopper out of the sink, but the water just stands there. "Stopped up *again*," she mumbles.

"You hear me, woman?"

"If I bring you home a Big Mac, will you promise to settle down?"

"I'd rather have Taco Bell. Why don't you get a job at Taco Bell?"

Pamela walks fast to their bedroom. "I got to get going."

Bobby follows her. She's slim, and he's always liked the way she walks. In their bedroom she looks through her purse. "I've got to get going," she says again.

"I do, too," Bobby says, grabbing her and pulling her down onto the bed. He gets on top of her.

"I have to go to work," Pamela says as though she's worn out.

Bobby pins her wrists on either side of her head, not to hurt her, just to keep her from getting up. He's wearing a sleeveless T-shirt and notices how skinny his arms are. He's been meaning to buy a set of barbells.

"Let me up."

She closes her eyes, and he notices for the first time this morning how pretty she is. When they were in high school, she was a cheerleader, and he knew she thought he was shit. He kisses her.

"Okay, can I get up now? I'm gonna be late. I might really have to go to work at Taco Bell if you don't let me up."

"I'm sorry I scared you in the kitchen."

"I hear they put dog food in their tacos."

He kisses her again and lets go of her wrists so that he can fondle her, and she pushes him away and gets off the bed. She looks in the dresser mirror and straightens her uniform and pats her hair back into place.

"One time when I went to Cincinnati," Bobby says, lying on the bed, watching her, "I saw a guy in a porno movie that kept talkin' about hittin' home runs and had a dick about as long as a goddamned baseball bat. I thought about that guy yesterday when Lon come here, sniffin' 'round like all these years hadn't went by and you wasn't married to me."

"I'll see you tonight. If I don't work a double shift, you want me to bring you a Big Mac for your supper or not?"

"Pam, I wanta ask you one thing before you go."

"Well, hurry up."

"Did Lon have a thing as big as a baseball bat?"

Pamela walks out of the bedroom. Bobby hears the front door open and slam, then the Maverick grinding and grinding and grinding, until it finally catches.

With "The Price Is Right" on, Bobby sits on the sofa with newspaper spread on the coffee table and cleans his gun. When he's done, he goes into the bathroom, brushes his teeth, shaves, and smears deodorant under his arms. He does body-builder poses in front of the mirror. He doesn't look all that bad, he thinks. He sure as hell would rather be skinny than fat. Big guys die young. Then he puts on a clean T-shirt, and he's ready to go see Becky Diane.

Bobby has gotten to like the freedom of his days. He doesn't look at want ads much anymore. He used to fill out job applications for factory jobs and construction work all over southcentral Ohio and even in Kentucky a couple of times, although he considers Kentucky a hillbilly dumping ground and the worst state in America, except maybe for West Virginia. He applied for a lot more jobs than he told Pamela he did. He didn't want her to know how many people were turning him down. It was better to have her think he was lazy.

When he filled out an application at the office of a man who owned a construction company, Bobby got the idea of becoming an antique-toy dealer. In the waiting room old toys sat in display cases. When Bobby asked the secretary about them, she pointed to a rusty little truck and said, "The boss paid two hundred dollars for that thing. I wouldn't give you a dime. But he loves those things. He dusts them off himself. Won't even let me touch them."

"Two hundred dollars?"

"That old beat-up thing over there, that tricycle—that cost him three hundred and fifty."

"Jesus H. Christ."

Driving into West Union, Bobby has his gun under the front seat. Every couple of minutes he reaches down and touches it.

He pulls his '69 Dodge Dart into a parking space in front of the courthouse. Becky Diane works in the driver's-license bureau.

A farmer in overalls, who looks around eighty, is trying to read the eye chart. Bobby stands in the doorway. The farmer can't get any of the letters right, and Becky Diane says, "No, Harold. Let's try one more time." She always asks people to read the third row of letters. Bobby wonders why the people in line who can't see don't just listen to the people in front of them and memorize the line: A Z B D E L.

The farmer guesses wrong again. "I'm sorry, Harold," Becky Diane says, "but I can't renew your license." She talks loud and slow, and the old man is bent toward her, frozen. "But there's an eye doctor in Peebles that'll sign a paper for you, and you bring it here, and I'll give you your new license."

Becky Diane smiles when she sees Bobby. She's thirty-five, ten years older than Bobby, but she still lives with her mother. Becky Diane is wall-eyed and has bad acne scars. She's thin except for a little bit of a potbelly. The first time Bobby took her to the Route 33 Motel, three months ago, she couldn't stop shivering, and she bled on the sheets. Bobby licked her belly and said, "You sure you don't have a tumor or somethin'?"

Last week she announced to Bobby that she'd been doing sit-ups and said, "Doesn't my stomach look a lot flatter?"

Today, during her lunch hour, they drive to a hollow outside of town and park. He shows her how good he's become with his pistol, shooting holes in the trunk of a skinny maple tree. Then he lets her shoot. She flinches each time she fires and can't hit the big tree she's aiming at. "This is hard," she says. "You're really good."

He unbuttons her blouse and cups his hands over her small pointed breasts. "You ain't like other women. If I wasn't married already, I'd marry you."

She strokes his face, and he kisses her fingers. Her hands are beautiful. Her fingernails are long and a different color every day. She gets manicures whenever she has her hair done, once a week. Her hair is thick and blond. Bobby has always heard men and boys say Becky Diane is a good-looking woman from the back. Last week at the motel he told her to turn over and get on her knees. He pretended he was with Christie Brinkley.

"I love you, baby," he says, and takes her hand and leads her to the car. He opens the back door, and she lies down with her skirt hiked up. He pulls her panties down over her shoes and buries his face in her neck. She makes little sounds that remind him of mice. When he's done, she wants to kiss, but he pulls back.

"I don't feel like it. Jesus, you're ugly." And he thinks about how pretty Pamela is.

"Why do you do this?" Becky Diane says, straightening her clothes. Bobby ignores her. "You do this all the time. We make love, and it's sweet and nice, and then you ruin it like this."

Bobby picks up his gun off the hood of the car and aims at a tree. He hears her sniffling. He pulls the trigger. Click. Then again. Click. He puts the barrel to his temple. Click.

When he stops in front of the courthouse to let her out, she's still crying a little. Her face is covered with pink splotches. After she gets out, she bends down to the window and says, "How about tonight? Can you get away? I'll tell Mother I'm going to the library."

"I might not be able to see you ever again," Bobby says.

"Why not, Bobby? Why not?"

" 'Cause I have decided to shoot somebody this afternoon. That's why."

He drives toward Peebles, where the McDonald's is. West Union is a dead town with shut-down stores, potholes, and a bunch of old loafers sitting around whittling. Peebles, though, always seems busy—a lot of cars and trucks, and besides the McDonald's, there are Taco Bell and Pizza Hut and the Big Boy drive-in restaurant.

On his way to Peebles he thinks about yesterday when Lon showed up. Lon was drunk and unshaven. He was driving a beat-up Pinto. Yeah, the big baseball star looked bad.

Bobby had been napping on the sofa. The trailer was cold from the air conditioner running all day, and all the lights were off. Bobby liked the idea of lying in the dark, chilly trailer, and drifting off to sleep, then waking up to find the afternoon and half the evening gone and Pamela due home soon.

Lon banged on the screen door and woke him up.

Bobby looked at him through the screen door and smelled beer.

"How you been, Bobby?"

Bobby nodded a few times, then said, "I been doin' good. Good. Pamela ain't here right now."

"I figured Pamela would be home since it's Sunday. My

daddy died, you know. Left me his farm. I just wanted to say hi to her."

"She's at work at McDonald's."

Lon nodded. "You know, this is the first time I been back to Ohio in six years. I been everywhere."

"You been to Hawaii?"

"No, but I been to most of the states out west."

Bobby nodded. "Yeah."

"My real estate agent says I might get nearly forty thousand for the place. Daddy didn't owe on it. I'm thinkin' of getting into real estate myself."

Bobby stared straight at him, but Lon was looking up at the sky. He kept looking up there. Then he shoved his arm through the flimsy screen and grabbed Bobby's T-shirt and said, "I can tell you exactly how she sounds when she's about to come."

Bobby got away and backed into the darkness of the trailer. "Don't you come in this house." He was shaking and bumped into the sofa. He sat down.

"House?" Lon said. "Shit."

"She told me you was crazy. She told me how you used to bust up your apartment after you messed up in games, makin' her think you was gonna kill her, and then tellin' your old man you was doin' great when he phoned you."

"I never once hit Pamela," Lon said, and hit the frame of the screen door with the heel of his hand.

"Said you threw things and punched walls."

"I never hit her, God knows."

"It was in the paper here about you battin' one-fifty. Everybody was talkin' about what a big disappointment you was. And nobody was real surprised when Pam come back home."

Bobby saw Lon reach for the door handle. He could have

come in but didn't. His hand dropped to his side, and he said,
"Bobby?"

"What?"

"Pamela has a big mole right next to her pussy."

"I know all about it."

"You goddamn hick. You never done anything or been
anybody."

For a minute the only sound was the chugging of the air
conditioner. It seemed awfully loud.

Then Bobby said, "Lon?"

"What?"

"She's growed a new mole."

"What?"

"She's growed a new mole. Right on the other side of her
pussy."

As soon as Bobby heard the door of Lon's Pinto slam, he
thought of his pistol in the nightstand in the bedroom.

# Nine

L on wakes up in his old room. Posters of baseball superstars are still on all four walls, yellowing and curling up at the edges. He opens the closet door and touches the sleeve of his high school uniform. He thinks about buying lightweight, colorful clothes and going to Miami to live and maybe become a vice cop. He likes "Miami Vice."

He drinks a New Coke for breakfast and looks at part of some new soap opera. Pamela comes to mind, and he says out loud, "Screw her."

After shutting off the TV, he starts reading volume six of the *New World Encyclopedia*. It's the only volume he still has, a salesman sample. He got into the habit of reading volumes of the encyclopedia when he was selling them in Oregon. Sometimes, when he didn't feel like bothering people, he would find a park or a playground or a shopping center and sit down on a bench and read his samples. He started by looking up famous baseball players. Pete Rose was in there. Then he started reading articles at random. He doesn't care what the subject is. He opens the book to any page. He wonders why he couldn't study when he was going to junior college.

He decides to drive into Peebles for lunch. When he passes the McDonald's, he sees a crowd of people inside. He goes down a couple of more blocks, then pulls into the Big Boy restaurant, where he can get curb service.

When the girl brings his order, she hangs the tray on his window and pauses after he pays her. "Do I know you?" she says.

Lon squints at her. She's wearing a stupid-looking cap with a fat boy on it holding a burger aloft. She has fiery orange hair, a pale complexion, and bright-red lipstick. Her T-shirt has the same fat boy on it the cap does.

"Do you?" Lon says.

"You just look familiar."

She's slim and her jeans are tight. She steps back, maybe so that Lon can see her better, and cocks her hips and puts her hand on her side.

Sixteen, Lon figures. Jailbait. But what the hell. "You might know me."

"No. I think I was wrong."

"I'm famous."

She looks at the Pinto.

"I didn't say I was rich."

"Yeah, well, I gotta go." She looks at him for a moment longer before she turns and walks back to the restaurant, her little butt performing for him.

While he eats his burger and fries, Lon watches her carrying trays to other cars. When she comes to take his tray away, he says, "Do I know you?"

"Sure. I'm famous," she says.

"I bet you're rich too."

"I'm the richest kid at West Union High School."

"You a freshman?"

"Senior in the fall. I can't wait to get out."

"I went there. Graduated a long time ago."

"You know that girl that became a movie star?"

"Yvonne Strickland? Those stupid horror movies?"

"Yeah, that's her name."

"She was before my time. I'm old but not *that* old. I graduated in seventy-nine."

"You oughta be able to apply for Social Security soon."

Lon grins. "I'm Lon Peterson."

"You a famous actor?"

"I was on the baseball team. Used to be a big picture of me all by myself next to the team picture in the trophy case in the lobby up there at the high school."

"That's you?"

"Is it still there?"

"Yeah."

"That's somethin'." Lon finds himself without anything else to say, and his eyes wander around nervously, but he feels happy. If nothing works out with this girl, it'll be okay; he can take her or leave her.

"Hey, I gotta go. Nice talkin' to ya." She turns and starts toward the restaurant. Then she stops and turns back. "But in that picture you sure look a lot different."

# Ten

Lunchtime is over. It's the quiet part of the afternoon at the McDonald's. Pamela isn't behind the counter, just a fat woman. Bobby looks at her name tag. "Hey, Betty Jo." He finds Pamela in the grill area, pouring a bag of frozen fries into a wire basket.

"You're not allowed back here," she says.

"I don't see what trouble I'm makin'."

"Ray said he didn't want you coming around here to see me when I'm working."

"Can I have some of them McDonaldland cookies?"

"If you pay for them." Pamela lowers the basketful of fries into hot oil, and the fries hiss.

"Lon hasn't been here to see you, has he?"

"No. Is that what you came to find out?"

"Damn, you're snappy. You know, sometimes I don't think you love me no more."

Ray walks in. "Bobby, what are you doing here?"

"I came to see my wife about a very important matter."

"Well, your wife is my employee."

"What does that mean?"

Pamela says, "It means, Bobby, that you're interfering with my work."

"I was gonna buy my lunch here."

"You don't buy it back here," Ray says.

"Okay, I'll leave."

"Thank you," Pamela says.

"But, Pam, I want you to always remember I love you, no matter what happens this afternoon."

Ray shakes his head. His face is red. Pamela looks kind of pale.

On his way out Bobby stops at the condiment center and stuffs his pockets full of straws and packets of ketchup and salt.

In his car he reaches under the seat and touches his gun. He should blow Ray away. He thinks of an antique dealer in Cincinnati: "Boy, most of this stuff you've been buying is junk. You've got to learn what's rare and what people want. You've got to buy things that are in good condition. Have you ever looked at a price guide?" Bobby should blow him away too.

The house Lon's old man left him sits far back off the gravel road. The long driveway is full of ruts. Bobby doesn't see Lon's Pinto anywhere.

The farm is quiet. The wind rustles the high grass around the house, which has lost most of its paint and gone a shade of gray that makes Bobby think of cancer.

The back door is unlocked, and Bobby enters the kitchen

with his pistol raised. The house smells like puke. In the living room beer cans are scattered in front of the TV.

In the hall he catches sight of himself in a mirror mounted on the wall: a skinny man in a T-shirt, his pants pockets bulging with straws and packets of ketchup and salt, a black gun in his hand; his hair is stuck to his forehead, and sweat slides down his red face.

He steps into Lon's bedroom. On the walls are yellowing pictures of baseball players. On the night table and the dresser and on a table in a corner are tarnished trophies.

Bobby opens the closet. Baseball uniforms hang there and a green suit. On the floor of the closet are stacked newspapers—the *West Union Gazette* and the *Adams County Courier*—with Lon's name in the headlines. Bobby lifts them, uncovering a stack of *Playboy* magazines.

Bobby remembers the way Lon was in high school. Stuck on himself. Lon never talked to him. Bobby heard he screwed every cheerleader in the school.

After laying the gun on top of them, Bobby picks up the stack of *Playboy*s. In the hall he sees himself in the mirror again—still sweating, even redder in the face, his arms full of pictures of naked women.

# Eleven

"You want something to drink?" Lon asks, opening the refrigerator and seeing only two cans of beer.

Cindy has walked on into the living room, checking the place out, and Lon feels embarrassed about the looks of the place. "No, thanks."

"Just as well."

"Your maid got the decade off?"

Lon goes into the living room. Cindy is looking at a painting of a clown on the wall. Lon did it from a paint-by-number set when he was ten years old. She's taken the stupid cap off, but she's still wearing the T-shirt.

Lon's palms are sweaty, and he keeps wiping them on his jeans. "You want to be my maid?"

"No way."

"I'm gonna be rich after I sell this place."

"So where are all these trophies you wanted to show me?"

"They're in here. This is my bedroom." She follows him in. "I grew up in this room."

She looks around. "Your trophies are tarnished. You should take better care of them." She glances at the narrow bed that has only a white sheet on it.

"I haven't looked at them for six years."

"I have twelve ribbons from gymnastics meets."

For what seems like a long time neither of them talks. The sun is setting, and the room is getting dark. Lon steps closer to her, and she doesn't move. "Hey, come here."

"I was just curious . . . ," she says, turning toward him.

He puts his hands on her waist and kisses her. Then she steps back and says, "Let's go someplace."

Lon has a feeling she's a tease. "We just got here."

"Don't let your blood pressure get too high, old man. You don't want to have a stroke."

Lon thinks about the word *stroke*. "So where you wanta go?"

"Star-Lite Drive-in. It'll be dark soon. You wanta take me?"

"What's on?"

"One of those *Friday the Thirteenth* movies."

"Okay. Why not? I'm a man of leisure."

When they drive past the McDonald's, he looks over. The place is almost empty and all lit up inside. The front has big windows, and he sees Pamela behind the counter.

"What's wrong?" Cindy says.

"Nothin'."

At the drive-in Cindy keeps calling kids over to the car

and saying, "Hey, what's happenin'?" and then introducing them to Lon. Lon feels silly. He nods at the kids and then ignores them, playing with his car keys. The girls all seem to have high-pitched laughs that grate on his nerves; the boys are all lanky and retarded-looking with peach-fuzz mustaches and goatees.

After the movie starts, whenever some dumb teenager is about to get his head split open or his guts ripped out (Lon thinks it's almost funny it's so stupid), Cindy clutches his arm and digs in her fingernails.

He tries not to think about Pamela, but she keeps coming to mind. He keeps seeing her behind the McDonald's counter. She was just standing there, staring straight ahead, at nothing, as if she were just waiting for him to drive by.

In the movie a cat gets chopped in half, and Cindy says sadly, "Poor pussycat."

Lon looks at Cindy out of the corner of his eye. Her mouth is open a little, and her eyes are wide, as if she's really into the movie. He turns his head and stares at her, but she doesn't seem to notice. The next time she digs her fingernails into his arm, he grabs her and kisses her on the mouth. Then he kisses her neck and holds her and won't let her loose.

# Twelve

Bobby calls Becky Diane and tells her to come to his trailer
tonight. Pamela is working a double shift.

Bobby and Becky Diane sit on the sofa watching a TV
show about near-death experiences. People talk about floating
above their bodies, watching doctors and nurses give them
shots, hang drug drips, and pound on their hearts. They talk
about rising a thousand miles a second, leaving the planet, and
being surrounded by warm, comforting lights, about seeing
dead relatives or Jesus.

When the show goes off, Becky Diane says, "Why do you
think some people are met by relatives and others by Jesus and
then other people see old friends or like that one man who saw
his second-grade teacher?"

"I want to be met by Marilyn Monroe."

"Do you think maybe you get met by whoever you want to meet you?"

"I'll tell you what I wonder," Bobby says. "I wonder what happens if you've been married about eight times like Elizabeth Taylor? Which husband will she end up with?"

"The one she loved the most, I bet."

"Yeah, I guess."

"My aunt Sylvia would want to be greeted at the gates of heaven by nobody other than Elvis."

"Yeah, I guess Elvis keeps pretty busy."

Bobby gets up and turns off the TV. When he sits back down, he sees himself in the blank screen, a tiny man far away.

"I knew you didn't mean it this afternoon," Becky Diane says.

"Mean what?"

"What you said about shooting somebody."

Bobby doesn't say anything for a minute. Then he says, "I decided to spare his life. But I could of shot him. He trespassed on my property and assaulted me."

"Who?"

"Nobody."

They both stare at the blank TV.

"Don't you want to do something?" Becky Diane says, putting her hand on his thigh.

"I grew up right across the street from her."

"Who?"

"My wife."

"Oh." Becky Diane takes her hand off Bobby's leg.

"I used to watch her goin' out with him, and I'd see him bring her home and them makin' out in his car in her driveway."

"Did you like her back then?"

"She come home from North Carolina, and she never wanted to see another baseball player or nobody that was like him. She hated him."

Becky Diane puts her hand back on his thigh. "I know she must be treating you bad."

"I got me some personalized license plates which said PAM-BOB." Bobby holds up his hands as if he held the license plate. "I'd never even asked her out. I just pulled up in her driveway while she was settin' on the porch so she could see how I felt. She thought I was crazy." He laughs.

"She must have been flattered."

"She married me, didn't she? I been married to her ten times longer than he ever was."

"Would you really marry me if you could?"

"What?"

"You said this afternoon you'd marry me if you could."

Bobby stares at the blank TV. Then he looks over at the kitchen table. "See them things?" Piled on the table are *Playboy* magazines, straws, and packets of ketchup and salt. "That's what I did today. I stole them things. And I spared a life."

## Thirteen

Pamela's feet hurt, and she hopes she can drive home without falling asleep. She pays for a box of McDonaldland cookies to take to Bobby. She's the last to leave. It's Monday night, but since it's summer, high school kids are out. A line of cars comes from the direction of Star-Lite Drive-in. Some boys yell at her as they go by in their growling car jacked up on tires three times too big. She ignores them. A few years ago she would have been flattered. Now she figures boys like that yell at every girl. They would yell at Betty Jo.

She gets in the Maverick and turns the ignition, and it grinds and grinds and grinds, then stops doing anything. Pamela rests her forehead on the top of the steering wheel. She thinks of the Camaro she saw on TV in Raleigh—years ago. For some reason that she realizes probably doesn't make any sense, she thinks that if she had bought the Camaro, she would be somewhere else now.

The Vampire said he really wanted to sell the Camaro that night. "Make me a reasonable offer," he said. "We're open all night. We don't sleep. We do get tired, though, and we sell cars at crazy prices."

Pamela hadn't made any friends in Raleigh. She met another player's wife when she and Lon first got there, but the other wife did nothing but brag about how her husband was probably going to be promoted to the Triple-A League soon—while Lon was dropping two or three balls every game.

"Late-night specials. Easy credit. You can be on TV," the Vampire said.

Sitting on her sofa, her legs tucked under her, Pamela thought about her mom—she had thought she hated her mom, but now she missed her—and about her girlfriends (some still back home in Adams County, others married and moved off to Cincinnati or Columbus or Detroit) and about all the boys who had told her they loved her: seven since she was thirteen.

She reminisced—as if it had been years and not months ago, just that spring in fact—about her and Lon making love in his Skylark. She would hold his face against her breasts and pat his sweaty hair and listen to his breathing and feel her own sweat trickle down her sides and feel herself slipping on the slick vinyl.

"Every preowned car has passed the safety-lane inspection."

She kept looking back and forth from the TV to the plastic clock on the wall. Lon was supposed to be back from a road trip that night. The clock was a bright-yellow chicken turned sideways. A relative of Lon's gave it to them for their wedding.

Parts of the movie had been boring so far. Some male

aliens needed women, ones with their minds sucked out. She picked up a copy of *Cosmopolitan* from the coffee table. Looking at magazines and watching TV were pretty much all she'd done since moving to Raleigh. In the mornings she watched Phil Donahue and reruns of "I Love Lucy" and "The Beverly Hillbillies" and game shows. When the noon news came on, she changed the station and watched four soap operas. She looked at *Redbook, People, Cosmopolitan,* and *Vogue.* At night, if the Rebels were playing at home, she had to go to the games. When the team was on the road, she began the evening by watching "The Newlywed Game," wondering how she and Lon would do. Then things improved because prime time started. Then late, if she couldn't sleep, the Vampire was on every night.

She had stopped fantasizing, when she looked at the pictures of beautiful women in beautiful clothes in the fashion magazines—had stopped fantasizing about being able to dress and look like them someday soon, had stopped fantasizing about Lon being in the major leagues, making a million dollars a year. She had stopped imagining that future because Lon was hitting .135 and dropping balls like hot potatoes. In the home games Pamela had gone to, Lon looked so clumsy playing third base, she was reminded of a retarded boy she knew back in Ohio.

In high school Lon seemed to float or glide around the bases after hitting balls so hard they almost instantly vanished. And there was the way he could crouch behind home plate—he had been a catcher in high school—for the longest time; his leg muscles were incredible.

All that grace and power—gone. Pamela wondered whether he might have suddenly gotten a brain tumor or something.

"These quality cars have been completely reconditioned by our trained mechanics. Drive your car off the lot and all the way to California. Worry free, I guarantee."

She was sleepy, but she didn't want to sleep. "How would I get there?" she said aloud, and realized she was talking about the Vampire's car lot. "Go to hell," she said to the clock. She could call a cab.

"Stay tuned for tonight's second feature, one of my favorites, *The Three Stooges on Mars.*"

She closed her eyes and saw herself getting dressed— jeans, blouse, shoes—then standing at the kitchen counter with a pencil and a pad of paper with yellow daisies along the bottom of each page, wondering whether she should leave a note.

Or tell him on TV. What would she say? "How would I get there?" And she realized she was talking about California.

She awoke, startled, a vampire on the TV, and she shouted, "Mom!"

She awakes, her forehead sore from where it's been resting on the steering wheel. She looks at her watch.

She groans, getting out of the car. She slams the door, then brings her fist down on the roof, but there's only a dull, soft thud. And she unlocks the McDonald's and uses the phone to call her mother.

# Fourteen

Lon hopes the beers will make his headache go away and give him some energy. He tries reading the encyclopedia, but the words keep blurring. When he turns on the TV, he feels he's had a bit of luck. On Channel 3 out of Huntington, West Virginia, the Reds are on, playing the Mets. Pete Rose is getting closer to Ty Cobb's record nearly every day. When Pete Rose comes up to bat, Lon shouts, "Go, Pete!" at the TV, the way he did when he was a kid.

He usually tries never to think about his summer playing for Raleigh, but after the Reds score a bunch of runs and he's feeling good—the day's not turning out so badly after all—he lets himself reminisce about one good moment: the time he hit his only home run as a professional baseball player.

The score was tied, and he hit the ball to the right-field

corner, where it took a funny bounce off the wall, off the huge face of a pretty girl drinking a Dr Pepper. The outfielder slipped. As Lon ran toward third, the third-base coach pointed to home plate and yelled, "Home, Lon! Home!"

But then the bad memories pour over him, and he lies facedown on the sofa. The Rebels ended up losing the game, partly because Lon bobbled a ball hit to him at third base. Why did they have to make him play third base? He was a catcher, had been a catcher ever since Pee Wee League. They said they didn't need another catcher; they needed a third baseman. That's probably what Johnny Bench was told, near the end of his career, his knees giving out. The one year Bench played third base, he was the worst third baseman in the National League. But Bench had always been the best catcher. Same damn thing happened to Lon. Best to the worst. Same damn thing. He always felt out of place at third base, never comfortable. Always felt like one leg was shorter than the other. Felt like the glove he wore wasn't his. And it wasn't. His was a catcher's mitt.

They said they were mainly interested in his hitting. But he couldn't hit. He dropped balls, made wild throws—and he couldn't hit.

He was suddenly a failure.

And being a failure was as mysterious to him as being a success had been. Hitting a baseball had come naturally; he could never explain it. He never thought about it. Then in Raleigh he thought about it all the time, the position of his feet, the angles of his elbows; people gave him advice, which didn't help.

All his life he had thought the hills, farmland, and small towns of Adams County were dull and ugly, but that summer in the South he yearned to be back home and to be back in high school, which he had just left. In his mind Ohio was all freshness and lushness; it was heaven compared with Georgia, Alabama, the Carolinas, and Florida—the redneck towns' ramshackle ball parks with tacky billboard pictures on all the outfield walls so that a baseball coming into the plate from the pitcher's mound got lost in the tooth of a smiling girl who used some goddamn special-formula toothpaste.

DRINK COKE. JOHNSON'S HARDWARE. VALLEY FORD.

Fuck them all.

One thing he felt he was learning was that only the present counted. Only in the present did you feel some thrill, some pleasure, or some pain. Memories didn't do you a damn bit of good.

He sits up on the sofa. He should get to work, he tells himself: fix the tractor; mow the fields; repair the fences; paint the house.

In a few minutes he stands up and goes to the back door and looks out. Then he walks to the barn. The big door is heavy and hard to open. Inside, it smells the way it did years ago. Hay and manure. The ghosts of pigs and cows and chickens are everywhere. The red and gray 1947 Ford tractor sits in here. By the door are an old baseball and a bat.

He takes them outside and swings the bat a few times at imaginary fastballs down the middle of the plate. Then he drops the bat and tosses the ball above his head and makes basket catches bare-handed. "Willie Mays," he says. He tosses the ball as high as he can, and it sails behind him and comes down on the roof of the barn. While it skates down the roof, he runs to the side of the barn to catch the ball when it drops from the overhang.

When he comes back to the front of the barn, a little red car is turning into the driveway. Clutching the ball, he runs to

the house, slams the door, and locks it. He goes into his
room and sits under the window, breathing hard. He hears the
car crunching the gravel. When it stops, he peeks out. A
Chevette. There's a knock at the front door. Then another.
After a couple of minutes he hears footsteps going around the
house.

He glances at the open closet and notices his stack of
*Playboys* is gone. "What the hell?" he whispers and looks
around. Nothing else seems to be missing. He thought for sure
he saw that stack of *Playboys* in there only yesterday. He
knows he did. He lifted one and looked at the cover for a second, then put the newspapers back on top of the magazines.
So . . . ?

"Lon!" he hears Cindy call. "Lon!" He sits still. "Lon!"
She's circling the house. "Lon!" Her voice is drifting off toward the barn.

He wants to stand up and holler, "Go away!" But if he
does, he knows she won't. She'll want to talk. She'll ask him
questions. *What's wrong? Did I do something? What about
last night?*

Jesus, last night.

There he was like some damn kid—at the drive-in movie,
in the backseat, sucking on a young girl's nipples. She said she
wouldn't go all the way. "I'm jailbait for you, old man." She
kept resnapping her jeans.

They were drenched in each other's sweat. Strands of her
hair kept getting in her mouth and his. There were beer cans
and oil cans on the floor of the backseat, oily rags, a McDonald's bag full of garbage. The smell was bad. "I'm not dumb
enough to let myself get pregnant," she said.

Jesus. Jesus Christ. Just like high school. They almost always gave in eventually. Especially if you pulled a rubber out

of your wallet and told them you loved them. Cindy, though, just wanted to French-kiss and pull on his dick.

Finally he came all over his jeans and her hand. And a fog lifted, and a cold draft slid up his spine, and he was mad. But at the same time he was glad he hadn't screwed her. He was tired as hell.

"Lon! Lon!"

He peeks out again, and she's standing by the driver's door of her Chevette, about ready to give up.

Lon looks at his closet again.

# Fifteen

**P**amela and her mother are at the kitchen table, drinking coffee.

"You're gettin' crow's-feet around your eyes already. You want a bottle of Oil of Olay? I got about twenty bottles when West Union Drugs had their going-out-of-business sale. You remember that? About three years ago, not long after your dad passed away?"

"Mom, I'm trying to talk serious here."

"I know, hon. I was just noticing those crow's-feet, and I thought to myself, 'She really is unhappy.' "

"I don't want to live with Bobby anymore."

Ruth stands up and takes her coffee cup over to the sink. She runs water and rinses the cup, then hangs it on a mug tree. "Who told you?" she says with her back to Pamela.

"Told me what?" Pamela asks, annoyed, thinking her mother is talking about something that has nothing to do with her and Bobby. She rubs the tablecloth with her fingertip. It feels greasy and has the smell of new plastic. Pamela remembers sitting here and cutting out paper dolls. She remembers coming home from dates and finding her mother sitting at this table in the dim light, looking up from a magazine and smiling a phony smile, giving her the once-over for undone buttons, wrinkled blouse, flushed face. Now her mother looks for wrinkles in her face. "Told me what?" Pamela says again.

Ruth comes back to the table and sits down. "About Bobby. You mean you don't know?"

"Know what?"

"Well, they always say the wife is the last to know."

"Who's he fooling around with? Jeez, he doesn't even have a job."

"Becky Diane Walters. That girl that works at the driver's-license bureau."

"But she's *ugly*. Ugly as sin. She's so ugly, she could be on television."

Pamela's mother gets a sad look in her eyes, and Pamela thinks about her father. He got cancer and smelled up the house for months, but when he died, Pamela's mother was as hysterical as a woman who loses her husband suddenly in an accident or at the hands of a crazed killer.

"I'm sorry, hon, about Bobby doin' this to you." Then Pamela's mother surprises her. "You shouldn't give him up to her. If he really cared for her, he'd have left you."

Pamela shakes her head hard. "But, Mom, I don't want him."

"Maybe that's what he senses. Maybe that's why he went

to another woman to seek satisfaction. Did you refuse him bedroom privileges?"

"Bedroom privileges?"

"The only thing she's got in common with you is she's a woman."

"No, Mom. You don't see. He's been playing around with this gun he bought, and he acts like a child half the time. I can't rely on him for anything, and I don't think he's ever going to get a job."

"I thought he was always real sweet to you."

"Well, he was in some ways. Sometimes. Sometimes he's all right." It's true. Sometimes he laughs out loud at the TV, has supper ready for her when she gets home from work, and gives her gifts—cute stuffed rabbits and mice and bears; a coffee mug with *Superwife* painted on it.

"He ever hit you?"

"No. But he aims that gun at me."

"When it's loaded?"

"No, but still . . ."

"He's just playin', then."

"What? He could kill me." Pamela blows out a long stream of air and feels her face flood with hot blood. "Why are you defending him?"

"I just don't think you ought to rush into another divorce. Now, I didn't say a word when you left Lon after only a few months."

"I didn't know you liked Bobby so much."

"It's not a matter of me likin' him or not likin' him." Her mother looks toward the windowsill where a plant sits. "I gotta remember to water my vines."

"Mom."

"Hon, you're twenty-four years old, and you've been married twice already."

"I know, Mom. Mom, I've been trying. I wanted it to work. I feel like something must be wrong with me. But I just don't know what to do."

"Well, you can't keep gettin' married all the time."

"You don't have to worry about that."

Pamela's lying upstairs in her old room when the phone rings down in the kitchen. The furniture in her room is white with blue trim, and all her old dolls are on shelves her father built. Her father was the only man who ever entered this room. She always told her brother she'd kill him dead if he ever set foot in here.

"Pamela!" her mother calls from the bottom of the stairs.

"Yeah."

"That was Bobby again. I told him you were asleep."

"Okay."

It's Pamela's day off, so she doesn't have to deal with McDonald's today. She wonders whether Lon has stopped by there. All day yesterday she expected to look up and see him.

An image comes to her: Lon sitting on the sofa like a zombie in their apartment in Raleigh. He wouldn't talk. He just stared. At nothing.

Once, she picked up one of her *Vogue* magazines, threw it at him, and yelled, "Stop feelin' sorry for yourself and *do* something. You feel *so* bad. For God's sake." And she paused, not wanting to go on but knowing she would. "When you dropped that ball today, some bald man in front of me said, 'Don't he look like a retard?' How do you think *I* feel?"

Lon got up and slapped her.

He never hit her again, but he'd throw lamps, chairs, and

knickknacks. When she yelled at him to stop, he'd say, "I'm just tryin' to *do* somethin', bitch!"

But if his father called, Lon would say, "Everything's fine. I got a cold, but I'll get over it." Then his father would want to talk to her, and she'd have to pretend too. Toward the end of the summer she left whenever Lon's father called. "I am not here," she would mouth to Lon as soon as he said, "Hi, Daddy," and she'd walk to the drugstore and buy something little, cotton balls or toothpicks or Band-Aids.

Every morning when Lon was not on a road trip, he reached for her and said, "I'm sorry, babe. I love you. I'll be okay."

At the end of the season when he was released by the team, he said to her, "I need you more than anything in the world."

But by then she had made up her mind.

Fits of violence. Fits of crying. Fits of love. She was sick of them all.

# Sixteen

Ruth watches Johnny Carson as she leafs through the August *Ladies' Home Journal* and sips a Pepsi (a real one, not a diet one), which she knows she shouldn't have, considering the weight she needs to lose, but it's a small pleasure, and sometimes small pleasures seem to be all that hold her together. Like now. Pamela is upstairs in her old room, determined to leave another husband.

Ruth usually doesn't stay up this late, but she can't sleep. She wishes Pamela could have at least picked another time, waited a month or two or something. Ruth hasn't gotten over her son, Darrell, leaving for the army. He just graduated from high school in May. She tried to talk him out of joining, told him about Uncle Ibra, who was killed in World War II, and Cousin Ellen's boy, who died in Vietnam. But the army had those commercials on during the ball games and "Saturday Night Live" and on MTV, which Darrell could stare at all day and night. "There ain't no war, Mom," he kept saying.

If Glen were alive, he would have said, "What the hell else is the kid going to do?"

The house still smells of Glen's cigarettes. At least Ruth *thinks* she still smells them. Maybe she'll ask Pamela whether she smells them too. When Ruth sees an actor in a movie about the fifties or sixties with a pack of cigarettes rolled up in the sleeve of his T-shirt, she thinks of Glen because he used to really do that. When they rode around in his Mercury and she leaned against his shoulder, he'd say, "Goddamn, don't smash the smokes."

Sometimes Ruth thinks she hears Glen snoring or coughing and looks toward the bedroom, then remembers he's dead.

The day she married him, in the receiving line at the church her mother whispered to her, "You're a fool."

Well, maybe she was. She was only sixteen, but she made the best of it. She and Glen stayed together. Nowadays, she thinks, everybody gets divorced at the drop of a hat. She and Glen had their rough times, a lot of fights even the first year.

Glen fixed cars and talked about becoming a race-car driver. He came home to their little shack of a house with engine oil gleaming on his face and his eyes flashing in the sexiest way. He had sideburns like Conway Twitty's, and he was horny every minute of the day. That was nice. But then there'd be some fight. He'd say her cooking tasted like shit, or she'd ask him to help with a load of laundry and he'd say, "Are you crazy, girl?" or he'd want to go out with some couple Ruth thought were trash. Or they fought about money. They always fought about money.

But they got through it. They stayed together. Even the times she suspected him of seeing another woman.

At midnight, just as Johnny Carson is introducing somebody she's never heard of, Ruth goes out to the porch and looks up the street, then beyond the house across from hers, the house Bobby grew up in, and sees mountains. She says a prayer for her daughter and Bobby.

Bobby grew up right over there with just his mother—there were all kinds of stories about his father: he was dead; he was in prison for life; he'd run away with a teenage girl. Four years ago Bobby's mother married an old man who was about seventy-five (she was maybe fifty at the most) and moved to Toledo.

Bobby wasn't a bad boy. He's not a bad man either, Ruth is certain. Pamela is hard on men.

Ruth looks up the street again, then at her watch, the way she did when Pamela went out on dates. Maybe she was too hard on Pamela back then. She was always acting like some old woman when she was only thirty-three, thirty-four years old. Back then, when Pamela was in high school, Ruth sometimes realized she acted like her own goddamn mother. She interrogated Pamela about dates and friends and said things to her like "You better start worryin' about something besides what you see in that mirror, girl."

But Ruth was looking in mirrors a lot herself. It was a bad time, one of the times Glen might have been seeing someone, the time Ruth came closest to walking out. "I'm a mess," she would say to her reflection, leaning toward it and touching her face with the tips of her fingers. She was thirty pounds overweight (and still is) and half consciously made her appearance worse by wearing polyester clothes from Kmart, as if she'd decided that better clothes would be a waste of money on a body like hers. If she had worn flower-print dresses and had had short hair in tight curls, she would have looked just the way her mother did when Ruth was sixteen and crazy about Elvis Presley because he looked so nasty and so sweet. She used to cut pictures of him out of magazines and hide them in a drawer under her panties and bras.

Seven, eight years ago—a bad time.

She'd stay up late, like tonight, unable to sleep, maybe waiting for Pamela to come home from a date. Glen would be snoring his head off. She'd look in their bedroom at him sprawled on his back, his big belly sticking up above the rest of him, the sheets in a pile on the floor because he always kicked them off.

One night, waiting up for Pamela, she went into the bedroom and lay down on her side and gently shook Glen and said, "I love you." He opened his eyes for a moment and stared at her, then rolled over onto his side. "I love you," she repeated.

A harsh cough exploded from deep in his throat. "What the hell?" he muttered. Then he sucked in a long snore.

She sat up, and she realized it didn't matter—she didn't mean it when she said she loved him. At least not at the moment. Love came and went. That's what she had learned in seventeen years of marriage.

His back was broad, strong-looking, somehow cruel-looking, but he never hit her, not once. The women on either side of their house had been hit by their husbands, they had told Ruth. The woman in the tacky pink house on the corner called the sheriff on her husband one time, making a scene for the entire street to gawk at. Sometimes she wished Glen *would* hit her. She wasn't sure why. Anyway she didn't want to think about such a crazy notion.

Glen didn't hit her, and Bobby hasn't hit Pamela. Pamela should be thankful, Ruth thinks. Pamela said Lon hit her.

Ruth never did like him. He had a head so big, he couldn't fit it through the front door. He used to sit out front in his old car and honk his horn. Rude.

When Pamela started dating Lon, Ruth started going into Pamela's room when she was out, entering cautiously, as if booby traps might be set. She sweated. She was careful not to disarrange things. She opened drawers, gingerly lifted socks and bras. If she had found something, she would have died.

Found what? Drugs? Birth control pills? A flask of whiskey?

Snooping reminded her of things God hated—the things she grew up feeling guilty about: everything from wearing eye liner to cussing.

She looks up at the stars and lets her breath out slowly. The moon is full. Ruth wonders how many nights have been exactly like this—the temperature around eighty, the stars shining, crickets singing, that smell of grass and trees? It could be a night ten years ago. Twenty. Twenty-five: Elvis singing a love song, the taste of Rolling Rock beer on Glen's lips.

It's just funny, the way the weather is the same, as if it should have changed along with everything else. Maybe when she gets older, she'll convince herself it has—like her aunt Marie, who claims she remembers when it regularly snowed three feet at a time in the Ohio Valley.

Ruth goes inside her house and presses the buttons on the cable box to find something to watch. She ends up with MTV. Sometimes it hypnotizes her, although she doesn't like many of the songs or musicians. She does like Bruce

Springsteen, though. He reminds her a little of the way Glen was when he was young.

She feels a pain in her chest and belches. That slut Madonna is on. Ruth feels awfully lonesome.

She looks toward the bedroom as if she were going to see Glen lying in there. "He's dead. Remember that," she says.

During that bad time—seven, eight years ago (has it really been that long?)—she was always lonely. Surrounded by Glen, Pamela, and Darrell, but always alone. She got a little crazy. She thought she was in love with her dentist.

Dr. Scott was a tall, distinguished-looking man who had gray temples and whose breath always smelled of liquor. Once, as he was leaning over her, peering into her mouth, he told her she had beautiful eyes—so large and so green. She felt her face burning. She started having dreams about him.

She went to him every month with some phony complaint. Once, she took him a plate of her homemade chocolate-chip cookies. While she sat in the waiting room, she noticed on the wall, among the pictures of animated teeth and smiling children holding toothbrushes, a picture of a cookie with an *X* drawn through it. Then Dr. Scott came in and said hello. She told him the cookies she held were not hers; they belonged to a friend; she was just taking them somewhere for her friend. . . .

When she had some little bit of surgery done and Dr. Scott put her to sleep, she woke up with the sensation that her breasts had been fondled. She tried to tell herself she was just fantasizing.

One night while she waited for Pamela to come home from a date, she wrote love letters to Dr. Scott, which she destroyed, burned on the stove top, after reading over once.

Then she heard a car in the driveway, and she hurried out to the porch. As she stood there peering at Lon's Skylark, she realized her robe was open, and she pulled it closed and tied the belt.

She couldn't see Lon or her daughter until Pamela opened the passenger's door and the car's interior light came on. Lon's face looked gruesome in the pale light; long shadows seemed to hang from his eyes.

As Lon backed out and then roared away, Pamela came very slowly up the walk, not looking at her mother, up the steps to the porch and into the yellow light.

Ruth said, "Did you have a nice time?"

"Why are you out here?"

"I was just getting some air. That TV is enough to make anybody feel like they're choking."

"The TV's not on."

"I just turned it off," she said as she took Pamela's bare forearm. Although Pamela resisted for a moment, Ruth led her over to the porch swing and made her sit down. They sat close, and Ruth studied her daughter, who stared at the street. Ruth leaned toward her, looking her over carefully, sniffing her, as if she could pick up the scent of male hands.

# Seventeen

It starts pouring down rain in the afternoon, and the lightning knocks out the electricity. Bobby wakes up when the air conditioner goes off, the fan making a rattling noise as it slows down. The trailer is dark. "Pam?" he says. All he hears is rain on the roof.

He gets off the sofa and looks out a window. Then he takes off his shirt and socks, dropping them on the floor, and goes into the bathroom and gets the shampoo. It's yellow shampoo with two percent egg, the cheapest Kmart sells.

Outside, Bobby bows his head and gets soaked. Thunder cracks nearby. His jeans get heavy with water. Then he steps against the trailer and lathers his hair. He likes the smell of the shampoo, and he likes the smell of the rain. He likes the way rainwater makes his hair thick and soft.

He bends over, letting the rain rinse his hair. It starts to hail, and he feels little needles all over his back and head. Small hailstones gather at his feet. Then it's just rain again, and he goes back inside the trailer and dries his hair with a towel and takes his jeans and underpants off.

In the bedroom he looks at himself in the full-length mirror on the closet door. The closet is across from the bed so you can watch yourself while you screw.

When he and Pamela looked at trailers, he noticed that most of the new trailers had a lot of mirrors in the master bedroom. Red wallpaper and big mirrors. A couple of trailers had mirrors on the ceiling over the bed. At first Pamela didn't like the mirror on the closet door because it made her feel funny, she said, like she was on TV or something.

When they first got married, they never missed the TV show "Dallas." They called each other Mr. Ewing and Mrs. Ewing because the characters Pamela and Bobby Ewing on the show were deeply in love. Pamela got tired of the show after a couple of years, but Bobby kept up with it for another season. Pamela would sit at the kitchen table and write letters to friends who had moved away, but occasionally she'd nod toward the TV at a new character and say, "Who's that?"

The electricity has come back on, and Bobby tosses his wet clothes in the dryer. The dryer turns the whole trailer into a steam bath. He and Pamela haven't been using it much the past year because the washing machine broke down. Pamela's been taking the laundry to her mother's to do. It's a lot cheaper than buying a new washer or going to the Laundromat, and her mother helps her.

Bobby thinks his and Pamela's sex life has been hurt by the breakdown of the washing machine. When the washer went into its spin cycle, the whole trailer shook. Bobby got into the habit of turning on the washer, even if it was empty, when they were about to have sex. It was like having a Magic Fingers machine built into their bed. Bobby got good at adjusting the washer and timing the progress of his and Pamela's sex.

Still naked, Bobby goes into the spare bedroom and looks at his antique toys. He likes handling them and thinking about how kids played with them long before he was born, how they grew up in worlds a lot different from his, how they are really old or dead now—and that's kind of weird for some reason.

He used to have a sign up by the highway saying ANTIQUE TOYS FOR SALE, but the mobile-home park manager made him take it down. She's a short, chunky woman with short hair streaked black and gray, and she has a bald spot on the back of her head. It looks like somebody puts a bowl on her head and cuts her hair with shrub shears. She's a nasty old bitch, and Bobby thinks somebody ought to blow her away.

He gathers up some of the old toys and carries them into the living room and puts them by the front door. He makes several trips. Then he gets dressed and combs his hair. It's soft and thick.

Outside, the sun is shining. There are puddles everywhere, and birds are all over, catching worms. Bobby puts the toys in the trunk of his Dodge and drives into West Union and is waiting at the courthouse when Becky Diane gets off work. He shows her what he has in the trunk.

"What are you going to do with them?"

"I'm gonna give 'em away."

They drive across the Ohio River into Kentucky.

"Why are you going to give them away?"

"I just got to thinkin' about how a lot of poor kids don't have toys to play with."

"You're sweet, Bobby. But aren't those toys worth a lot of money?"

"A small fortune."

"Well, can you afford to just give them away like this?"

"I'm gonna get a job."

"Where? Do you have one lined up?"

"Not yet. But I'll get one. I got to. She didn't come home last night."

"Your wife?"

"Who else?"

"Do you know where she is?"

"She went to her mom's house."

"It really is nice of you to give your toys away." She lays her hand on his knee.

"I always have felt sorry for people that don't have."

"That's—"

"Like you."

Bobby pulls onto a dirt road, and in a minute they're in the middle of a cluster of shacks, the hamlet of Sadiesburg. Little dirty kids with long, stringy hair are playing in the road. Bobby pulls over, gets out, and opens the trunk.

"Hey, you kids. I got some toys for you."

They gather around, slowly. The adults stand in the doorways of the shacks, their eyes narrowed and their arms crossed. Becky Diane stays in the car and rolls up the windows.

A man steps out onto his porch and spits a stream of tobacco over the porch rail.

Bobby starts handing out toys, smiling. Right away a boy says, "This ain't nothin' but junk," and spits.

A girl says, "Ain't you got no *new* toys?"

Bobby says to her, "See, honey, these are real special toys. You could sell 'em someday and get a lot of money for 'em."

He touches the girl's shoulder, and she jumps back. "Don't."

The man on the porch spits another brown stream, then says, "We don't need none of your junk, boy."

Bobby dumps the rest of the toys on the ground and gets in the car.

"What those kids say?" Becky Diane asks.

Bobby drives away fast, kicking up big clouds of dust.

"Did they thank you?"

"They didn't say nothin'."

"What's wrong?"

"Nothin'."

"What they say? I had the windows up."

"That's why you're all sweaty. Why the hell you do that?"

"What's the matter, darling?"

"Shut up."

They're quiet for a minute.

Then Becky Diane says, "Forget your wife. She doesn't deserve you."

Bobby pulls off the road into a ditch full of high grass. The car is slanted way sideways. Bobby takes hold of Becky Diane and kisses her hard and squeezes her breasts. A pickup truck goes by.

"Bobby! It's broad daylight."

"I don't care."

"I'm afraid the car's going to tip over in this ditch the way you got it."

"It won't."

Another pickup truck comes by. It slows down. An old farmer takes a look, and Bobby gives him the finger.

"Let's wait till we get to your place. And I'll make you supper."

"No," Bobby says, getting off her. He starts the car. "I got some things to do. I'll drop you off at the courthouse."

When he gets home, he calls Pamela's mother's house, and her mother tells him Pamela went out.

"Think she'll be sleepin' again the next time I call?"

"I don't know, Bobby. I wouldn't push her right now if I was you. Let her think about things."

"Tell her I'm comin' over to see her later tonight. Tell her I love her."

"I'll give her the message."

It's a little after seven in the evening. Bobby gets his .22 pistol out and loads it and walks out to the woods behind the trailer park. Three boys about ten years old are playing back there, and he tells them they'd better stay clear, but he lets them watch him shoot at the cake pan. He wonders whether Pamela is out somewhere with Lon. He hits the pan every time.

"You're good, mister," says one of the boys. "Can I try?"

"This is a dangerous thing. Better not."

"You ever shoot birds?"

"Nope. I happen to like birds."

"I bet you could hit birds if you shot at 'em."

Bobby squints at the kid, lets his head fall sideways, and says, "I know I could."

# Eighteen

After working on it a full day Lon gets the tractor started. For the next two days he mows fields, repairs fences, and slaps paint on anything that needs it. At night he drinks beer, reads the encyclopedia, and watches TV. He's glad he doesn't have a telephone.

Cindy comes by three times. He hides twice, once in the hayloft of the barn; the other time he runs back into the woods. The third time he has gone into Peebles for paint and motor oil. She leaves him an apple pie from the bakery section of the Kroger supermarket, along with a note saying, "I just thought you might like this. Maybe I'm wrong. Love, Cindy."

Lon can't make up his mind about whether he should see her again. She's a nice-looking girl. But she's not as pretty as

Pamela was in high school or still is probably. He didn't get that good a look at her when he went by the McDonald's the other night. He has never had a woman or girl as pretty as Pamela, although he's had his share of good-looking ones. He should go to see her at McDonald's. Then he won't have to mess with Bobby. But showing his face to Pamela isn't easy. She might hate his guts, for all he knows.

He thinks sometimes that letting himself lose her was the biggest mistake of his life, but when he had her, he was always wanting other women. He loved Pamela, but he had to be realistic, practical, he used to tell himself when he was a baseball star. He figured that after he made it to the majors, he wouldn't be the same man she married, the simple farm boy full of dreams; something would happen to him. He wouldn't divorce her, but she would have to give him a certain amount of freedom. He often fantasized about nameless models on the covers of women's magazines he saw in grocery stores and about women in *Playboy*. He liked to conjure up images of some actresses on TV. He had thought he might meet some of those women someday, and nobody could say what might happen.

He would smile at pretty girls, wink, strut, and say, "You're lookin' mighty fine, honey."

He loved the way they giggled. He could tell from a girl's giggle whether she would let him have her. He had good instincts. He just knew, the way he knew how to hit a baseball—until he lost his instincts in Raleigh. All that summer in North Carolina, when he saw a pretty girl, he blushed and ached deep inside in a way he'd never known before.

And he actually let Fred Potts, a teammate, talk him into going to a whorehouse. They were on the team bus going back to Raleigh, and the inside of the bus was dark and quiet, silent as death because the Rebels had lost twelve of fifteen games on the road trip.

Lon stared out the window at the black sky and the blacker houses and trees and barns. Fred Potts, who was sitting directly behind him, broke the silence when he started singing: "I get off on fifty-seven Chevys, I get off on screamin' guitars . . ." Potts was thirty-four. Lon had heard that Potts played in the majors for three weeks once, years ago. In the game that day he had doubled and dropped a ball. Lon had dropped two.

Somebody told Potts to shut up.

He stopped singing, but hollered, "Boys, we all need to take a little road trip—out to a whorehouse I know." Potts waited for responses but got none. So he sang again, "If I told you you had a beautiful body, would you hold it against me?"

Somebody yelled, "Fuck you, Potts."

"Yeah, now you're talkin'," Potts said, then sang, "Had me a girl in Kansas City, she had a scar on her left titty. Had me a girl in Kalamazoo—"

"I said fuck you."

Potts put his hand on Lon's shoulder. "How 'bout it, boy?"

Lon turned his head. "Potts, I haven't seen my wife in two weeks."

"What? You weren't seriously thinkin' of goin' home to the old lady, were you?"

Suddenly Lon realized that Potts's offer wasn't so bad. Going home and facing Pamela wasn't going to be a party, that was for sure. She had dreams, and he was destroying all of them. He knew she didn't want to hear about his aching teeth and headaches and stiff joints. How one leg felt shorter than the other. He'd gotten three hits in ten days.

"Hey," Potts said, "you know what the difference between a wife and a job is?"

"I think I heard it before, Potts."

"After five weeks a job still sucks."

"I thought it was 'five *years.*'"

"Nope. Five weeks."

When the bus reached the ballpark in Raleigh, Lon didn't walk home. Instead he followed Potts to his car.

While Lon rode in Potts's beat-up Nova, heading toward a whorehouse out in the country, he thought about something the Rebels' manager had said to him that day before the game, which was the worst possible time to say anything to a ball player trying to get mentally ready to perform. Lon realized, while Potts's tape deck blasted with some hillbilly's wailing, that whenever somebody started a sentence with, "I'm not saying . . . ," the person was always going to say what he said he wasn't: "I'm not saying you're a bad ball player. . . ."

A slump had to end sometime, Lon told himself. He had hit a couple of balls hard the last two games, but fielders made great plays. His luck was bound to change. Soon he'd hit one hard, and nobody would catch it; he'd hit a broken-bat blooper, and it would fall in. He'd get used to playing third base. Yes, he'd adjust.

Then the truth swelled in his head and pressed at the backs of his eyes; he gnashed his teeth, and something in his gut pulled loose and sank into his bowels.

Sometimes slumps never ended. Sometimes you didn't get well—you just died.

Potts turned into a dirt driveway. The so-called whorehouse was an old farmhouse sitting far back off the highway, the grass in the yard high and full of weeds and wildflowers. The headlights of the Nova caught the biggest dead tree Lon had ever seen, a black monster reaching down to take the house in its grasp and crush it. Pigs squealed when the car pulled up to the back of the house.

While Potts banged on the screen door and shouted, "Hey, Sara!" Lon stood several feet behind him, trying to see the pigs he could only hear.

"You woke me up, you son of a bitch!" a woman yelled. She stood in the doorway, dim yellow light behind her.

"Did you miss me, baby?"

"It's five extra for waking me up."

"Your sister here?"

"Why?"

"I got a friend."

"Where?"

The porch light came on, illuminating a small patch of yard. Lon stepped into the light and nodded at the woman. Small-breasted and pale, she wore a green silk robe. Her brown hair hung limp to her shoulders.

"This is Lon," Potts said. "He's a ball player too. A real superstar and a real stud."

"Come in the kitchen while I see if I can wake up Mary Ann."

When he sat down at the kitchen table, Lon pushed two empty beer bottles away from him and toward Potts and whispered, "There's only two women?"

"How many you need, boy?"

"You said it was a whorehouse."

"House." Potts gestured, making circles with his hands. "Two whores." He pointed at the ceiling.

"They got diseases?"

"Who cares?"

"They raise pigs on the side?"

Potts just looked at his own hands lying on the table.

Sara called from upstairs that they could come up. She met them at the top of the stairs and told Lon to go to the room at the end of the hall.

"Thank you," Lon mumbled as Potts and the woman disappeared behind a door.

The house smelled like old people—dust, mothballs, and medicine. He walked slowly, thinking he could leave, take Potts's car, and be home with Pamela in half an hour. He knocked, and a woman told him to come in.

Lon stepped into the room and nodded at her, relieved that she wasn't ugly. She was on the bed, stretched out and naked—a thin blond girl about his age with a tattoo of a rose beneath her navel. She yawned and stretched, her breasts trembling, the muscles in her arms and legs defining themselves.

"I'm Lon."

"Oh. Well, what you want me to be?" she drawled.

After the girl turned off the lamp next to the bed, the room was black. She didn't talk. Her breathing was soft. She touched him gently. Lon wondered only for a moment, at the very start, what he'd tell Pamela, not just about tonight but about the last two weeks. The last two months. He had no idea.

The girl raked her fingernails down his back, something one of those cheerleaders at West Union High liked to do.

It was so dark, he had trouble for a moment determining whether his eyes were opened or closed. It was black either way.

Then the girl started to whine, and he felt sweat bloom on his back. Her fingers did a dance.

And he saw a slim, nameless, perfect woman. Then she became a different woman, also perfect. Then another.

# Nineteen

It's always busy between eleven and one, but today the lines seem longer than usual, and Ray's yelling, "Let's move it. Y'all move like a bunch of cows."

Right after Pamela fills an order for ten cheeseburgers with regular fries and small Cokes for a lady with an army of kids, she looks up and sees Lon standing in her line. She can't remember the last time she had her dream; it's been several days at least. She hasn't been dreaming at all, she doesn't think. Not since she left Bobby.

A fat woman orders, and Pamela says, "What?"

The woman's face turns red. Pamela always screws up with somebody who will be mean about it. The woman puffs her cheeks out, sighs, and repeats her order. She has long black, lusterless hair, and Pamela imagines bugs scurrying around in it. Out of the corner of her eye she sees Lon behind the woman, like a bug coming out of her hair.

Pamela turns around, reaching for burgers and fish, some wrapped in paper and some in Styrofoam boxes that come down narrow slides from the grill area. She crushes a box a little, not meaning to grip it so firmly, but everything feels light and slippery, hard to hold. She puts three boxes and a large Coke on the counter.

The woman glares at the boxes, then glares at Pamela. "I didn't ask for no fish," she says. "I hate fish."

Ray pops his head through the door leading from the grill area and yells, "Hey, you're tryin' awful hard to be stupid today, aren't you?"

The fat woman smiles at him, and he smiles back.

Ray's only a year older than Pamela, and they went to high school together. She hates having to take his crap. Turning to get the correct order, she feels the building tilt. The lights brighten. Thoughts stampede: If they were in high school, she'd ask a boyfriend to beat the shit out of Ray. She takes in a long, deep breath. Bosses should always be old men with white hair you naturally feel respect for. Ray tried out for baseball one year in high school and didn't make the team. Pamela was a cheerleader. She used to be married to the greatest baseball player in the history of Adams County. She wants to yell that fact to Ray, and she even gets her mouth open, but then realizes she wouldn't be making much sense.

Lon steps up to the counter. She keeps her eyes on the keys of the register and says, "Welcome to McDonald's. May I take your order?" She smells beer.

"I just wanted to say hi." He belches.

"Your order, sir." She remembers how he can be a real fool when he's drunk.

"My daddy left me his farm."

She looks behind her. Everybody's grabbing at fries and burgers and shouting orders. She turns back and sees her line growing. "You gotta order."

He says something in a soft voice, and with all the noise she can't hear what it is.

Ray's voice, high and strained, yells, "Hey, what's goin' on on Number Two?"

Lon says something else she can't hear.

"You want a hamburger, okay?" She grabs one wrapped in paper off a slide and shoves it into his hand. "Fifty-five cents, please."

"Don't you want me?" Lon says.

"You're drunk."

"But—"

"Fifty-five cents."

Lon hands her a dollar and turns away. She doesn't try to give him his change.

A farmer in overalls steps up and gives her his order. She loses sight of Lon after he goes out the door and turns, weaving, his shoulders stooped. She looks at the farmer, who's staring at her. "What?" she says.

Later in the afternoon when Ray disappears for his rendezvous or whatever, Pamela says to Betty Jo, "I'm leaving. When Ray gets back from screwing his girlfriend, tell him I'm sick. Tell him I puked all over the place. Tell whatever you want to."

Walking out to the parking lot, Pamela wonders what kind of woman would want to fool around with Ray. He's skinny, bones sticking out all over, and has orange hair, the color clowns have. And he has no idea of how to dress. This morning he came in wearing red polyester pants that were too short.

When he sat down, she could see his shins above his droopy brown socks. She imagines a fat, pasty-looking woman, somebody like the fat woman with the buggy hair, in a dingy little motel room, telling Ray he sure is sexy, to get those red polyester pants off before she tears them off. Fat. Pasty complexion. Or maybe Ray's woman looks like his wife. Frail, flat-chested, hairy arms. Ray's wife brags that her husband is *the manager* of McDonald's, as if that were some prestige job: chief of surgery. Hell. Chief of fries.

Pamela is driving her mother's Buick. The mechanic at Texaco told Pamela that the Maverick needs about six hundred dollars' worth of work. She would rather just buy a new car. She has allowed herself to fantasize about Camaros and Trans Ams, but she'd be satisfied with a Ford Escort if it ran. She thinks she'll sell the Maverick as junk and get whatever she can for it.

She drives down Highway 33 and just keeps going. She has a full tank of gas, and for a few minutes she thinks she needs nothing else. She can keep going. She can be in Pittsburgh before dark.

After forty minutes she ends up in Portsmouth. She passes the Holiday Inn where she spent her first honeymoon. The sign says, CONGRATULATIONS JUDY AND MIKE. She thinks about going to a movie and feels anger well up because she starts thinking about how she and Bobby have never been able to afford cable TV. A few months ago she said to him, "Everybody else in the world has cable."

"You think those starvin' kids in Africa have cable TV?"

"You're missing the point." She looked at the rusty toy truck he was holding. "You must have rust for brains."

"You got McDonald's grease for brains."

She parks on the street, near a movie theater. She walks

up to it and looks at posters advertising the movie currently showing. It's an old theater. She's been in it and remembers water stains on the high ceiling and rips in the plushy seats and big stains on the thick carpet. Elegance gone bad.

When she sees old movie actresses on TV talk shows or in commercials or in made-for-TV movies, she almost cries. She wonders whether they sit around watching their old movies, amazed by how beautiful they *used* to be. She thinks about how she's going to get old, and she can't believe the way her life is turning out, has turned out.

The posters show cars smashing into each other and explosions and the hero and heroine kissing, their shoulders naked.

She recalls the smell of the theater, stale popcorn and something cold, musty. She remembers the beam of light in the darkness and Lon's hot breath in her ear, his fingers exploring her crotch, Clint Eastwood blowing somebody's brains out.

When she saw Lon today, she was surprised by what she felt and didn't feel. He looked different. Washed out, smaller, older. He wasn't anything like the beautiful man or the horrible man of her dream. She remembers she once loved him, but she can't recall what love feels like. He wasn't frightening either. A few times she had had wild fears of him coming into McDonald's and shooting her. There are always stories like that on the news. She was surprised that he just walked out when she treated him cold. The drunk fool.

She walks down the sidewalk, not paying attention to other people until a teenage boy sitting on the step of a pool hall says loudly, "I want a Big Mac, large fries, and a Coke." She turns at the next corner, walking fast, self-conscious about her McDonald's uniform now. She thinks everybody must be looking at her. Wearing her uniform on the street is like going out in public in pajamas.

Finally she stops, sweaty, her legs aching. She's by a low concrete wall that separates the sidewalk from the bank of the Ohio River. The river is a couple of hundred feet away. On the other side of the wall, in the mud, are cigarette wrappers and beer cans and condoms.

She looks across the river at Kentucky. Mud and shacks and mountains. She looks up the river, toward Pittsburgh, then down, toward Cincinnati. There are no boats.

She drives toward Pittsburgh. The highway turns north. She sees billboards advertising motels and restaurants in Steubenville. What if she just kept going, disappeared? She thinks of a tabloid headline she saw recently: ALIENS KIDNAP MOTHER OF TEN. *A mother of ten.* Jesus, living with aliens might be easier, she thinks as she turns the car around and heads for home.

Nearing West Union, Pamela feels lucky that Bobby hasn't come to her mother's house to see her. Lucky—but also disappointed and surprised. She wonders whether he really cares about that ugly woman. Pamela glances at herself in the rearview mirror. Crow's-feet.

When she gets into West Union, she stops for gas. Her mother will say something if the tank is empty: *Where in the world did you go? You know how dangerous it is for a girl to drive all over creation alone? You never know who's a maniac. I read that mass murderers are usually smart and handsome.*

After getting the gas she heads for the mobile-home park. She needs to go to her trailer and get some of her things— makeup, clothes, her radio. She imagines herself carrying those things into an empty apartment with bare white walls, a place where she will live alone. But when she gets to the entrance of the mobile-home park, she can't make herself turn in. She just can't do it. She's going ten miles an hour, and a pickup truck honks, then speeds past her, honking again. She doesn't look over. Picking up speed but planning to turn around any moment, she feels as though she's been away from her home, that crappy little trailer, for a long time.

The tires screech, and she turns around in a farmer's driveway. When she passes the trailer park again, she takes a good look. Everything looks somehow different, the trees, the utility poles; the colors of the trailers seem to have faded. Everything looks older, more run-down.

Returning home from a long trip, she thinks, you're always afraid you're going to find your home ransacked and burned to the ground. The trailer is old and crummy, but it's home.

She ends up all the way back in town and turns around in the lot of the Kroger supermarket. The sun is almost gone. It barely winks above the hills. She heads back toward the trailer park. She has to do it. She has to get her things and face Bobby.

She remembers a vacation she took with her parents when she was nine. As they were pulling out of the driveway, her mother said, "Well, the place will probably be ransacked when we get back." Then four hours later her mother said, "I wonder if I turned that burner off on the stove. I was heatin' some water for my coffee. I think I did. Well, anyway, we've got insurance. If the house is burned down when we get back, I guess I'll get to buy that new sofa I've been wanting."

Pamela worried the entire trip about her clothes and her dolls and her goldfish. She wouldn't eat much, and at motel swimming pools, when other children talked to her, she'd say, "Your house ever burn down? You think *everything* burns up?"

At the end of their vacation, nearing home, she said to her father, "I don't wanta go home."

"Christ, girl," he said, "the whole trip you've been wanting to know when we were going home."

It was true. She had wanted to go home, to see whether it was still there. But now she didn't want to face the ashes. Her charred dolls. Her dead goldfish. As they turned onto their street, she hid her eyes behind her hands, and her mother said, "What in the world is wrong with you?"

The sun drops behind the hills, and Pamela turns on her headlights. She slows down and puts on her turn signal, although no one is behind her. It occurs to her that she should tell Bobby to get out, that she wants to live there. She can't live with her mother—that's for sure.

Bobby's Dodge is parked next to the trailer. The license plate says PAM-BOB. The first time she saw it was over five years ago. She was sitting on the porch of her parents' house one day in early April, and Bobby's Dodge came down the street, but instead of pulling into his driveway, he pulled into hers. He shut off the engine and sat there. She said hi from the porch and waited for him to get out of his car. He didn't. Pamela looked down the street and saw the Mister Softee ice-cream truck coming for the first time that year. Not until after she saw the truck did she hear its bell. Two small kids ran out to stop it. Then Pamela looked back at Bobby. She was getting mad—he was *so* weird—and was about to go inside when she noticed the personalized license plate. She liked the fact her name was first.

"Why did you do this?" she said, pointing at the front of his car.

He opened his door, got out, walked around to the front bumper, and pointed. "This ain't no joke. I think you're the most beautiful girl I ever seen."

It's gotten dark suddenly. The night is cool and clear, but the window air conditioner is chugging and dripping. Stars bleed their light across the sky.

Some of the residents of the park are sitting outside on lawn chairs, drinking beers or Cokes. Edna, Pamela's elderly neighbor, is sitting in a circle of light from her porch lamp. She raises her scrawny arm and nods her head. "You and Bobby been on a vacation?"

Pamela just says no and opens the trailer door. She flicks on the light and thinks for a minute that she must be on TV or in a dream. The air in the trailer is icy. A can of gun cleaner sits on the coffee table. The colors of everything are unnaturally bright, like on "Miami Vice." Bobby is sprawled on the floor in a pond of blood, his head blown apart.

# Twenty

Almost as soon as Becky Diane gets to work, the sheriff's secretary, Rita, comes into the license bureau. People have started to line up for their eye tests, but Rita says, "Becky Diane, honey, you got to come with me. Right now. This is real important."

"What's the matter?" asks Becky Diane.

"Just come with me."

Becky Diane follows Rita down the hall, noticing how fat her rear end is, and into the one women's rest room in the entire courthouse. Becky Diane has often wondered whether the builder assumed that the only women using the courthouse would be a handful of secretaries, that lawyers were men, judges were men, juries were men, and criminals were men.

Rita says, "Honey, you better lean against the sink 'cause I got some bad news for you."

Becky Diane figures Rita's going to tell her some gossip about somebody who works at the courthouse. Rita's always the first to know about people's operations or divorces or money problems. "Okay. But I can't stay away long. I have people waiting to renew their driver's licenses."

"Now, don't you get yourself excited. Just let me tell you the best way I know how." She pauses.

"Yes? Yes?" Becky Diane has always been afraid of getting into trouble at work, although she never has in sixteen years.

"See, the sheriff got a call last evening about . . . an incident."

"An accident?"

"An incident. Well, yes, an accident. Maybe. See, it was about Bobby."

Becky Diane's heart lurches. "Bobby? Bobby who?"

"Your Bobby."

"*My* Bobby?" Her heart goes into a sprint. A sweat breaks on her forehead.

"Honey, he killed hisself. Shot hisself through the head. Nobody knows if he done it on purpose or not. His wife said he was always playin' around . . . Honey, are you listening?"

Becky Diane hears a roaring sound, like a huge seashell placed against her ear. The sink she's leaning against is cold.

"You take the day off. You hear?"

Becky Diane turns around and twists the faucets. The water pressure is weak, and the water merely dribbles out.

"I want you to know," Rita says, "I don't judge people. I say live and let live. I know you must of really cared about him. I know most people around here don't understand that."

"Around here?" Becky Diane looks up from the water and at her reflection in the mirror. "Who knew?"

"Honey, everybody in town knows you and him were havin' an affair."

Becky Diane hates the way she looks, hates herself for being ugly, and wishes Rita would stop staring at her.

"Everybody knows?"

"Sure, honey. You and him ran around in broad daylight. What do you expect people to think?"

She doesn't know what she expected people to think. She didn't know they would be spying on her and speculating about her. She never kissed Bobby in public or held his hand. She and Bobby could have been just acquaintances. Or friends. Men and women are allowed to be friends. Aren't they? But, no, everybody assumed something dirty was going on. So what if there was. Those people still had no right to think so.

Then the tears finally come to her eyes and spill down her cheeks, and she looks worse than ever, but what does it matter? She notices that the mirror is filthy.

"Honey, I'm goin' down to the bureau and tell all those people they'll just have to come back some other day. Don't you worry about a thing. You hear?"

Becky Diane feels Rita's hands squeeze her shoulders and feels Rita blow a sigh against her back. Then Rita leaves. Alone, Becky Diane looks up at the high, white ceiling.

# Twenty-one

Pamela hasn't seen Bobby in a suit since the day they got married. They had a small wedding at the First Baptist Church, which his mother attended regularly. Only a couple of Pamela's girlfriends from high school came. Although they had all graduated just a little more than a year before, most had moved away to cities to find jobs and husbands. The girl who had been maid of honor at Pamela's first wedding had moved to Oregon and had never written. Bobby's best man was his mother's boyfriend, George. Some of the guests mentioned to Pamela that they thought it was nice Bobby picked his grandfather to be best man. Pamela didn't bother to try to straighten them out.

Bobby borrowed the suit he wore from a guy he knew at the feed mill he worked at, but the guy didn't come to the wedding. The suit was too big, the sleeves so long only Bobby's fingertips stuck out; the pants legs bunched around his shoes. Standing in the receiving line, he kept having to pull his sleeve up to shake hands. Pamela's father got a grip on just Bobby's fingertips, and Bobby's arm flopped like a dying fish.

When she told her father she and Bobby were going to get married, he said that she would have been better off staying with Lon and helping him through his hard time, and even if he couldn't play professional ball, he could have gone to college (hell, anybody could go to college) and become a high school coach, and their life wouldn't have been bad.

Now Bobby's wearing one of her father's suits, a brown one. Bobby doesn't look like himself, even though the undertaker plugged the hole in his head. The undertaker also gave him a haircut and put makeup on him. She's standing by his coffin, a line of people behind her, waiting to take a look. She knows that everyone expects her to take her time, so she stares and stares.

She didn't want an open coffin or even a funeral. She wanted to have him cremated, but her mother said that cremation was a horrible thing and that she certainly hoped Pamela wouldn't stick *her* in a furnace when she passed away.

"Bobby didn't pass away," Pamela said. "More like he blew away."

"You don't know what you feel after you're dead. That's why I object to it."

They were sitting in her mother's living room the morning after Pamela found Bobby. The TV was on because Ruth thought it would help them feel that things were normal. But she didn't think a soap opera was a good idea, so she had "Love Connection" on. A man was talking about the horrible date he'd had with a woman who did nothing but talk about how rich and good-looking all her old boyfriends were. She also went to the rest room every five minutes: "I mean how can you have a conversation with a person who gets up to go to the john when you're in the middle of a sentence?"

Pamela looked away from the TV and said, "You don't feel anything when you're dead. That's what being dead means."

"You know, your great-grandmother always claimed her husband came to see her after he died."

Since her mother said that, Pamela has been thinking about ghosts. She doesn't know whether she believes in them or not. When her father died, she didn't give a single thought to ghosts, but if they do exist, she's afraid that Bobby is the kind of weirdo who would want to haunt people.

She looked at "Love Connection" for a minute, then said that Bobby would like being cremated. "Maybe I could do something romantic, like pour his ashes in the Ohio River."

"That river's filthy," her mother said. "I hear people been catching catfish that have tumors."

"Maybe I'd want to keep his ashes on a shelf in my home."

"I hear they give you a little carton like something you get at a Chinese take-out place. Aunt Ellen had Uncle Dilbert cremated and kept him in a vase on a coffee table, and one time a visitor used it as an ashtray."

Pamela gave in. "Okay." But she was thinking, *If I cremated him, I could flush the son of a bitch down the toilet.*

Now as she stands by Bobby's coffin, she feels like crying. She feels sorry for him looking so unlike himself. Her mother said people cry at funerals not for the dead person but for themselves. Sometimes that's true, but Pamela knows she's crying now for Bobby and for Bobby's mother, a short, scrawny woman Bobby looked just like. She's standing next to Pamela, and her face is red and wet and rubbery looking. Next to her, his arm around her as if to keep her from falling over, is old George, whose face is wrinkle on top of wrinkle.

# Twenty-two

For two days Becky Diane has stayed in her room. She told her mother she has the flu, knowing her mother wouldn't get close to her for fear of catching it. Her mother read somewhere that sometimes when people over sixty get a bad case of the flu, their bowels blow up. But every few hours she brings Becky Diane a bowl of chicken noodle soup and some crackers, placing the tray by the door, knocking, then hurrying down the stairs.

The only man Becky Diane ever loved or was loved by is gone. The son of a bitch is gone. He loved her mind, her hands, her elegant neck. She is certain he really loved her. He had a pretty wife, but he wanted her, Becky Diane.

Gone. "The bastard," she whispers. She has never cursed,

but now she mutters words Bobby used constantly. "Dork. Dipshit. Motherfucker."

For two days now she cries and she cusses and she sleeps. When she wakes up, she opens the door of her room and finds a cold bowl of chicken noodle soup.

# Twenty-three

One night in August a storm blows the barn over. Lon hears nails and boards screaming like ghouls in movies. He wonders what his daddy felt when he was lying on the kitchen floor dying. At least his mama had people around her. The house shakes when the barn lands. An atomic blast.

In the morning he takes a look at the giant wreck. He drives into Peebles and knows there are other pay phones but decides to use the one at the Big Boy restaurant to call the real estate agent. He figures the agent ought to know about the barn and can maybe give some advice, but Lon gets an answering machine. He just hangs up.

Lon has come to realize that when he gets depressed, he thinks a woman will make things right. But even if he gets hold of a woman at those times, she doesn't help for long. It's like getting drunk. Still, he can't stop feeling the need and looks around for Cindy. He asks a waitress, and she tells him Cindy has the day off. "I don't think she wants to see you," says the waitress, who is pretty, better-looking than Cindy.

"I never met a female that knew *what* she wanted."

Driving home, he tries to remember what it feels like to make love to a woman, but it seems he can't really remember except in dreams. Most of the time he dreams about Pamela. Sometimes Gina, a waitress he knew in Oklahoma. She was older than he was and had hard, defined biceps from carrying trays for thirteen years and scars on her ass where, she told him, her ex-husband, a real bastard, used to bite her so hard she bled. Oklahoma was a void but for Gina. Lon washed dishes and took to wearing a cowboy hat. Wearing his new cowboy hat and nothing else, he would walk around Gina's house, singing "Home on the Range."

"You're not a cowboy," she'd say. "You're a baseball player."

"I'm a cowboy now."

"You're a dishwasher."

"Just till I have enough money to buy some cows."

Gina. Her breasts bouncing as she crossed the bedroom, her nipples the color of bruises. Her black hair fanned across a white sheet. Her black eyes flashing. Her tongue flicking out to sting him with wet love.

Gina. Spitting on the bed. Her rump swaying as she ran out, shouting back, "Don't be here!"

Sitting on the bed, nodding, her dust drifting in from the driveway through the open windows, he put his finger in her foamy spit and raised it to his lips.

She had found out about him and the new cashier at the

diner. The cashier had a big nose, but she let Lon bite her ass and do a couple of other things he'd never tried.

He goes home and looks around at the mowed fields and repaired fences, at the freshly painted house. He's proud of what he's done. Inside the house he has hung cheap wallpaper that has vertical stripes and painted the bathroom, and he got the toilet to flush right and not overflow.

He looks at the collapsed barn and wonders whether he can sell the lumber. He needs money. A couple of days ago he sold some rusty parts of old farm machinery to an antique dealer. The man said city people would hang the stuff on their walls.

He sits on the sofa, trying to read his encyclopedia, but he keeps thinking about girls he's known: Cindy, Betty, Lois, Kathy, Gina, Debby, Mary Sue, Pamela, Ann, Lori, Jan. . . . He wonders how many women his daddy had in his life. Maybe only one. If Lon could find the right woman . . . Maybe after he sells the place, he'll go back to Oklahoma. He wonders where he can find Cindy. He wonders whether Pamela is living with her mother—he heard about Bobby.

Later in the afternoon Lon goes into Peebles again to call the real estate agent and gets hold of him this time, asks what's going on, why he hasn't shown the place, and tells him about the barn. The agent says he's going to put "Make offer" in the newspaper and the real estate catalog.

Lon goes to Pizza Hut to eat supper. His waitress is a sweet-looking brunette with a nice smile. She keeps asking him whether he needs anything, but his instincts aren't sending him a clear signal. She might be after just a good tip. In any case he decides he'd better keep his hands off her, or he won't have anywhere left to eat.

When he gets home, there's a pan of rubber dog shit by the door and a note from Cindy: "Hear you were looking for me. It's nice to know you're thinking about me. I've been thinking about you too. I've been thinking about how I thought I liked you. I was wrong."

# Twenty-four

Pamela talks to her baby—"I got us some ice cream, Pumpkin"—after she gets home from the grocery store and lifts the carton out of the bag, as if the baby were not inside her but waiting at home for Pamela's return.

Two weeks after Bobby killed himself, she found out she was pregnant. She'd been using her diaphragm without the cream because it was so expensive.

Sometimes she forgets about the baby, like when she's shopping, working at McDonald's, or watching something exciting on TV. She figures that when she gets bigger, she'll never forget. Then she'll have the baby, and her life will never be the same.

After she puts the groceries away, she watches "The New-lywed Game." She says, "That guy's getting old." She can't believe how old the show's host, Bob Eubanks, looks. She watched the show when she was little and always wanted to be on it, mostly because she thought Bob Eubanks was incredibly cute. Now he's getting gray, and yes, bald, too, she decides, although he combs his hair to hide it. Deep lines are etched across his forehead, probably from raising his eyebrows so much.

"What kind of car," he asks, "will your wives say, gentlemen, is best for making whoopee in?"

A skinny man with crooked teeth says, "A hearse." There go Bob's eyebrows. "It's long," the skinny man explains. "You can lay down in it."

"Oh. Okay," Bob says. He looks at the camera. The eyebrows spring up again. Deep lines.

"He used to look a lot different," Pamela says to her stomach, to Melinda or Matthew. She wants it to be Melinda.

She wonders how many of the couples on "The Newlywed Game" end up divorced. Some of them really seem to hate each other's guts.

When the show's over, Pamela sits on the porch and watches the traffic. The one-bedroom house she now rents is on the main strip of Peebles, close to the street and only two blocks from McDonald's, a good location since she doesn't have a car anymore. She sold Bobby's Dodge to pay for his funeral. Her mother wanted Pamela to live with her, but Pamela told her if she did that she'd miscarry for sure. Her mother cried. But that was last month, and her mother has brought over blankets—she says Pamela will freeze in this house when winter comes—and boxes of canned foods to show she cares and has forgiven the remark about miscarrying. Pamela feels a little like somebody on welfare.

Often the cars passing her house are going too fast and change lanes recklessly. "That guy drives like a nut," Pamela says to her baby.

She watches an orange Pinto go by. The driver is looking at her. She almost waves, then realizes it's Lon. In a minute the Pinto comes past the house again, but Pamela is inside with the door locked, peeking through a chink in the curtains.

Pamela watches a horror movie starring Yvonne Strickland. Yvonne went to West Union High School in the late sixties. When Pamela was a little girl, she heard about how Yvonne moved to California after she graduated, married a rich man, and acted in movies. Yvonne was the closest thing to a celebrity Adams County could claim.

*Satan's Touch* is about a young woman who sells her soul for eternal youth and beauty. Nobody in the movie can act, in Pamela's opinion, including Yvonne, who has on a miniskirt in most of the scenes, showing off her good, fleshy thighs. She has big breasts, too, but Pamela has seen prettier girls around Adams County; she considers herself prettier than Yvonne, whose blond hair is obviously dyed. Yvonne has on an awfully lot of dark eye shadow and fake eyelashes. The mole on her cheek looks painted on. Pamela doesn't think Yvonne made any movies after the early seventies. Probably got too fat.

When Pamela was growing up, Yvonne was better known in Adams County than any sheriff or mayor or criminal. Nobody had expected anything of her. Nobody noticed her until she showed up in a movie no one would have gone to if Yvonne's mother hadn't bragged to everybody that her daughter had "made it" in Hollywood. Then every girl in West

Union claimed to have been a good friend of hers. Boys claimed to have screwed her.

And Pamela thinks about how Lon was famous too. Everybody predicted he'd be making millions by the time he was twenty-five. She thought she'd be married to him forever—they were eighteen, and they would never die.

Then she remembers Lon, that summer in Raleigh, telling his father on the phone that everything was all right. At the time the lie made her mad; now it seems only pathetic.

Maybe she could have been more sympathetic, more understanding. When she came home from Raleigh, her mother said, "Did you support him the way a wife's supposed to?"

Pamela was sitting in her mother's living room, minding her own business, looking at a *Vogue* magazine. She threw the magazine down and said, "Hell with him. What about *me*?"

In *Satan's Touch* handsome men fall in love with the woman who has sold her soul. But they die instantly if they lay a finger on her or if she touches them. Pamela can identify—she, too, is bad news for men. Maybe she didn't love Lon or Bobby enough, although she remembers a time in high school when she would have gladly died for Lon. There was a lot more passion with him than with Bobby. She recalls sweaty nights in the backseat of Lon's Skylark, the way she felt out of control, always a little surprised, as her heart calmed, at the reappearance of the world: the sounds of crickets, cars in the distance squealing their tires, the rustling of trees. Her lips would swell from so much kissing. No other boy meant a thing to her. Now there's no one. No man who means anything to her. No interest.

At the end of the movie Yvonne's character is somehow freed from her contract with Satan, but she immediately ages about two hundred years. A young man who looks slightly like

Paul Newman still loves her. He holds her hideous corpse in his arms and cries.

Pamela remembers she found a gray hair on her head yesterday.

She has to get up at five in the morning to make biscuits at McDonald's. She feels sick and doesn't take a shower. "You go ahead and sleep some more," she says to her stomach. Sometimes she thinks about a movie Bobby took her to when they were first married: An alien from outer space raped a woman, and she gave birth to a monster that ripped its way out of her stomach. The monster was green and had big red eyes and fangs, and it sneered at its mother's bloody corpse.

At work Betty Jo is already mixing batter for the biscuits. She's brought in her ghetto blaster and is wagging her fat rear around, and Madonna is screeching about feeling like a virgin.

While the biscuits are baking, Betty Jo and Pamela go into the party room, which is furnished with bright plastic tables that look like lily pads and stools that look like mushrooms, and there's a plastic statue of Ronald McDonald. Betty Jo scratches Ronald McDonald's crotch and says, "That feel good, buddy?" She lights a cigarette and says to Pamela, "You don't look good. You're all pale."

"I'm getting the flu or something. *You* seem to be feeling pretty good."

"It's my birthday. The guy I live with says he's got something for me I'm gonna love."

"Happy birthday."

"Yeah, I'm thirty today. Hard to believe I made it this far. Dirty thirty."

Pamela thought she was closer to forty. "Congratulations."

"Yeah, dirty thirty. Hey, why don't you go on home? I'll tell Ray you're sick."

Pamela stays until about nine-thirty. Then she does leave, feeling achy, her head hurting. The walk home wears her out.

She watches the last few minutes of "Donahue," then goes into the bathroom to wash her face. She looks in the mirror at her pale face and dirty hair. Dirty thirty, she thinks. For a moment she can't remember how old she is. Twenty-four. Only twenty-four. She hears a game show come on the TV. She thinks she's found another gray hair when someone knocks at the front door. She takes her time getting it.

Lon is on the other side of the screen door. Pamela looks to make sure it's latched.

"I been meaning to come see you," he says.

"You saw me last night."

"Yeah, I saw you sittin' out here. But you know what I mean."

"Well, what do you want?"

"I'm sorry about comin' in McDonald's when I'd been drinkin'. I just wanted to be friendly."

"You want to come in?"

"Yeah, sure."

But she makes no move to unlatch the door. She just stands there, staring through the screen at his chest. He's wearing a white T-shirt that says "Van Halen" in screaming red letters.

Lon shifts his weight from one foot to the other. His hands are in the pockets of his jeans. "You don't look good," he says. "You sick?"

"I'm old."

"Hell, we're still kids." He reaches up and combs his long

hair out of his eyes with his fingers. "You know, they still got my picture in the trophy case at the high school?"

Pamela stares at the dirty pink slippers on her feet. She's wearing an old terry-cloth robe. A voice on the TV shouts, "Come on down!", and an audience applauds.

"Say, you gonna let me in so we can talk?"

She looks at Lon's face. He looks boyish, but when he smiles, nervously, the skin around his eyes cracks.

Then he looks off in the direction of Pamela's neighbor's house, at something Pamela can't see. He says, "I was wonderin' if we couldn't start seein' each other. I mean since Bobby's . . . gone." He waits. He squints at whatever he sees.

"I'm pregnant. Did you know that?" A dump truck rumbling past shakes the house.

Lon looks at her. "No."

"Well."

"Yeah, well . . ." Again he shifts his weight from one foot to the other.

She steps back and slowly swings the door shut.

# Twenty-five

Stacked all around her room—on top of the dresser, the small white desk, the nightstand, on the floor against the wall, stuffed under her bed—are books. Romances, mysteries, science fiction, and biographies of movie stars. Becky Diane stopped reading when Bobby came into her life. There didn't seem time, with meeting him places and talking to him on the phone and thinking about him. She loved to think about him.

Now she's reading again, three or four books a week. But some lunch hours, evenings, and Sunday afternoons she doesn't feel like reading. Instead she just wants to remember Bobby. In some ways, thinking about him is better than actually being with him, because she doesn't think about the way he was nasty sometimes and the mean things he said about people and the way he would pull out of her embrace or knock her hand away.

She thinks only about the times he touched her hair or face with the tips of his fingers and said things like, "You got real beautiful hair. And, you know, your hands could be in movies. I saw a woman on TV, and she made movies. Nobody ever saw her face, but her hands had been in twenty movies and a bunch of TV commercials."

She thinks about holding his hand while they sat on the trunk of a fallen tree in the woods, the sun coming through the leaves and dappling the ground around them. They watched squirrels and rabbits and birds. She doesn't remember the way he pointed his finger at them, aiming it like a gun.

# Twenty-six

September.
Sitting on the edge of the sofa, leaning toward the TV, Lon sees Pete Rose line a single to left field to pass Ty Cobb's record.

As soon as the ball drops, fireworks go off, and Lon wishes he had a color TV. Now he sees Pete's mom and his young wife, his second wife, who's holding her and Pete's baby, Tyler. The Reds players surround Rose. The older players who have known him a long time slap his back. The younger players shake his hand. Marge Schott, the team owner, a small, sturdy woman, shuffles out to first base and hugs him. The TV announcer says Pete's dad is probably looking down from somewhere above and smiling on his little Petey.

Lon sits back as he watches Schott present Rose with a

new Corvette—the excitement suddenly draining from him as it hits him that what Pete Rose has done does him, Lon, not a bit of good. He wonders why anybody cares what a baseball player does. But fifty thousand people in Riverfront Stadium in Cincinnati are still cheering their heads off.

He leaves the TV on, but he goes outside, picking up the old bat and ball by the door on his way out. It's only a few minutes after eight, and there's still some light, a hazy gray.

Lon looks in the direction of the neighbors' place, their shack and their car corpses, remembering those kids he gave his autograph to.

He takes a batter's stance with the bat in his right hand and tosses the ball as high as his eyes, then swings. There's a satisfying crack, and for a moment he sees himself in a filled stadium—his mama and daddy and Pamela sitting in box seats behind home plate.

And the ball sails over the collapsed barn.

# Twenty-seven

**P**amela sits on the sofa watching a game show, her whole body aching. Her belly is swollen, and her thighs are fat. She can press her finger into her calf and leave a dent. The game show's emcee is explaining that people interested in being on the show can write to an address in Hollywood, California.

She sees herself—thin, the top down on her Camaro, the wind whipping back her hair as she speeds across the desert, headed for the ocean.

Then she wonders why she couldn't have met a rich man, like Yvonne Strickland, and lived in California. She knows—as if it were something she had never known before—that she's going to get old. She wonders whether she'll ever be in love again—or believe she is, the way she once believed she was in love with Lon.

Desperate love.

The baby kicks.

# PART II

# 1991

# One

When she hears Lon turn on the shower, Crystal makes herself get out of bed. She sleeps in his old, faded high school baseball uniform, the pants legs bunched around her feet, the shirttails hanging to her knees. On the seat and knees are grass stains impossible to remove and over a dozen years old.

She shuffles down the hall past the bathroom where the shower roars, her feet bare on the cold hardwood floor, then on the tile floor of the kitchen, and she opens the cabinet above the counter next to the sink. Her eyes have trouble focusing. She sees spots. Her head aches. She thinks she's getting ulcers.

Wheaties. A box of Wheaties is what she finally sees. The first few days, when she came to live with Lon last month, she got up an hour before he did and made eggs and bacon and oatmeal and muffins. She worked cheerfully in the dimly lit, cold kitchen, goose bumps on her bare thighs because, at first, she wore only the shirt of Lon's uniform, the number 14 over her heart. But all that was ages ago—last month—and now she puts the Wheaties on the table.

In the refrigerator the milk carton is empty. She groans, notices a pickle jar with only pickle juice in it and a twelve-pack Pepsi box with no cans in it.

She shrugs, shuffles back down the hall to the bedroom, and pulls the covers over her head. If she weren't so sleepy, she might cry.

# TWO

She dreams of opening Lon's front door and stepping out onto the porch. Piled in the middle of the porch are hundreds or maybe thousands of chicken heads, the dead eyes dry and all of them staring at her, pleading with her for . . . for what?

She wakes up, sweaty, struggling for breath under the scratchy blankets, almost suffocating, it seems, before she finally escapes.

It is already noon. Winter light fills the old house. The wind howls; tree branches scratch at the windows. She feels guilty for sleeping so late, even though she has nowhere to go, nothing to do. She pulls on blue jeans and a sweater. Later she might even brush her hair.

On the kitchen table an empty beer can stands next to the

Wheaties box. She looks in all the cabinets for something that might interest her. There are Cheese Puffs and Fritos, some Cornnuts, a can of chili (extra hot). When she opens the refrigerator, she stands there awhile. She keeps seeing those chicken heads. A brick of margarine is mutilated because Lon has dug into the center of it with a fork instead of cutting pats off the end like a normal person. Chicken heads and exploding black stars swim around the empty milk carton, the empty Pepsi box, the empty pickle jar. Stars pop and fade. Crystal closes her eyes, shakes her head.

Then she hears a car on the road that runs past Lon's farm. She tenses up and prays it isn't the florist's delivery boy again.

Holding her breath, she waits for the sound of the car crunching gravel in the driveway, the squeak of brakes, the high idle of the car's engine, the slow, lazy, soft steps of the boy's sneakers on the wooden boards of the porch, then finally the loud, flat buzz of the doorbell that always reminds her of a fat boy in junior high who laughed hysterically at his own farts.

She doesn't breathe.

She imagines herself opening the front door and the delivery boy—his long, stringy hair completely covering one eye, holes in the knees of his jeans—holding out more flowers for her to take. And she would scream. She would scream like a girl in a horror movie she saw one time who discovered her boyfriend's head in a hatbox.

Crystal's husband has been sending flowers every couple of days since she moved in with Lon last month. The delivery boy leers and smirks every time—it is no use trying to tell her he doesn't, she has argued to Lon—and she figures everybody in the county knows Buck sends her flowers and knows all about what a bitch she is. She's surprised there hasn't been a story on the front page of the *Adams County Courier* about her.

Although she doesn't want the flowers, she doesn't have the heart to dump them in the garbage, even after they've dried up. So vases of flowers are all over this old farm house Lon rents—on the kitchen counters, on the top of the refrigerator, on the floor in the dining room (which doesn't have any furniture in it), on the end table in the living room. The ones on top of the old black-and-white TV are a month old, have become the brittle, black corpses of red roses.

Her lungs ache from not breathing.

Then miraculously, mercifully, the car passes by.

She closes the refrigerator. She takes a handful of Wheaties from the box, chews them, the flakes dry and scratchy in her throat. She has to do something before she goes insane.

She stares at the telephone on the wall. It's an old-fashioned black phone. She slips her hand under her sweater and fingers her navel, digs out some lint. Then the black, smooth receiver of the phone feels heavy in her hand, and her finger strains to dial a number she suddenly has to work at remembering.

She hears herself talk in a muffled voice that leaks through a roaring in her head: "Mom, it's me. I'm all right. But I . . . I need some money."

"Doesn't he . . . that man . . . work?"

"His name is Lon. Yeah, he works. He's a real estate agent, but—"

"Well, isn't he willing to give you anything?"

Crystal knows she has made a mistake. She should have called her daddy at his office. He probably wouldn't have even told her mother he gave her money. Crystal could have said, *Daddy, can this be our own little secret?* And she could have giggled like a child, and he would have said, *Sure, baby.*

But it is too late now, and besides, her mother's disgust at what Crystal has done is not as bad as her daddy's sorrow over it.

"I just want to go away for a few days," she says to her mother. "To think. I don't know what to do. I just want to go to Cincinnati for a few days, and I need money to stay somewhere. I need to get away. From here. From Lon."

"Does he mistreat you?"

"No."

"Does he beat you?"

"He's sweet as can be, but I can't think clear about things around him."

"I'll tell you what you can do." Her mother pauses. The phone crackles as if the call were long-distance.

"What?"

"You can stop being a selfish tramp and go back to your husband."

Crystal slams the phone down, something she has never done to her mother. For a moment she experiences a tingle of pleasure. She feels like a sexy, wild character on a soap opera.

Then the doorbell buzzes.

# Three

Late in the afternoon Crystal is watching a "Waltons" rerun when she hears Lon come in the front door. He says hi and goes into the kitchen and pops open a beer can. Then he calls, "These some more flowers from your husband?" She doesn't answer. She can't help hating Lon a little for never throwing a fit over the flowers; he would be jealous if he really cared about her. He says, "Where's he get all the money for these things?"

He comes into the living room and stands off to the side of the sofa so as not to block the TV. Crystal doesn't look at him. Olivia Walton runs out her front door and throws her arms around her long-absent husband and starts crying with joy. Mr. Walton has been working at a factory job over a hundred miles away in Richmond so that he can buy his family

Christmas presents. The horde of Walton kids gathers on the porch of their house, smiling, their faces glowing.

Lon drinks his beer. "Look like a bunch of idiots, huh?" he says. Then he looks at her. He rubs the back of his neck. "Are you crying?"

She feels her bottom lip tremble. Despite everything going on in her heart and mind, she wonders whether Lon ever wears anything to work but that old green suit of his.

"You crying over this stuff?" Lon waves his hand at the TV.

She nods, then shakes her head. She's crying but not over "The Waltons," not exactly. She looks at Lon, and although her tears make him blurry, she can see he is grinning.

"Ah, Crystal, there's nothin'—they're not even real people." Then he touches her shoulder—and that does it. That's all she can take.

She turns into somebody else, somebody insane. Her heart feels as though it's struggling to turn itself inside out. Her fingertips tingle. It just happens; she has no control over it, like the guy who turns into the Incredible Hulk.

"Olivia Walton!" she shouts.

"What?" Lon takes a step back.

"Olivia Walton would love that husband of hers if he lost both arms and . . . and his lips!"

"What?"

"The bitch!"

"But it's just a goddamn TV show," he says.

She springs off the sofa and rakes her long, pink press-on nails from his ear to his chin.

Christ, she can't just stand here, but she feels stuck in place, shaking, her vision dark around the edges. And Lon slaps her.

All of a sudden she's outside, her face stinging, the cold air making her shake worse. Hanging from the roof is an antique metal triangle for ringing men folk and children in for dinner. Next to it is a crank siren the farmer who used to own this place must have installed back in the fifties with the certainty the Russians would someday attack; the brand name, Banshee, has been half eaten by rust. Some part of her brain tells her the siren is what she needs, so she starts cranking. The sound is obscene. It is the sound of the world ending.

Then she jumps off the porch and flees toward the barn. And past it. She hears Lon call her. The rustle of the high weeds she's running through make her think of swarms of locusts. The sun burning low in the sky blinds her, and she trips over something, tumbles to the ground.

But she has found what she wants: the bomb shelter. She lifts the hatch, climbs down the ladder, pulls the hatch shut, and locks it, the dead bolt slipping into place with a clunk that sounds final, like something that can never be undone.

And here she is, in total blackness, with the throbbing of her heart filling her head. Oh, God, she needs to . . . to what? She can't see a thing. She feels her way around like a blind person. She needs to . . . She finds one of the cots. Yes. She needs to sleep some more.

# Four

When Lon wakes up, his head throbs from too many beers. As he rushes around, the floor seems to be alive, keeps throwing him off balance. He can't believe he slept as late as he did. Since Crystal moved in, he's been getting up early and leaving the house to make her think he has a lot of work to do, is a big success as a real estate agent.

He looks around for her and calls her name. Her car is in the driveway, so he figures she's still in the bomb shelter. Crazy. Just his luck to have a nut move in.

He drives fast into West Union to the open house he's hosting. He's been trying to sell the place for six months. "Nice starter home," Lon's newspaper ad says, which lets everybody know it's a cheap dump. "Big lot to add on third bedroom, second bath." He puts up signs at both ends of the street and borders the front yard with plastic flags.

As he finishes the flags, an old lady walking a poodle that looks as if it has cataracts pauses and says, "What a sight."

"Looks like Christmas, don't it?" Lon says.

"Looks like a car lot."

Another agent in town recently told him she always cooks a roast when she has an open house to make the place smell homey. Lon is experimenting today with a roast beef TV dinner.

While he waits for people to show up, he wanders from room to room, trying to get his blood flowing and his head cleared. All the rooms are empty except the kitchen, which has an oven and a refrigerator. He looks out windows. Although it's the middle of February, he mowed the grass on Friday, and the yard looks about as good as it's going to. All the trees died of Dutch elm disease and were cut down. There are half a dozen stumps out front and five in back. No trees mean no leaves to rake—he'll try saying that and see how people respond. Low-maintenance yard. But it's a big yard: low-maintenance *grounds*. Maybe, he tells himself, he'll try the line in next week's newspaper.

It's quiet. He hears the low roar of the flames in the gas oven and the shudder of the refrigerator when it shuts off. Houses still furnished and occupied are more interesting. Sometimes when he has nothing to do, he likes to use his lockbox key to go into people's houses and look through drawers and bathroom cabinets, to open jewelry boxes. He reads medicine bottles, touches women's dresses hanging in closets, looks at bill stubs and receipts. Sometimes he tries on suits. Once, he put on a cocktail dress just to see how it felt. If he knows the owners or if he ever meets them, he never says anything of course, but he always feels he has something on them, if only the knowledge that they are mere mortals.

Lon has on the dark-green polyester suit he got married in twelve years ago. The suit has lasted all these years. In a way he's glad it's been twelve years since that summer; he's slowly moving farther and farther away from the bad memories. He's walking away from that time in his life and only occasionally looks back. But he feels that, while he's walking, the years are rushing by like an express train, people's blurry faces at the windows, as though he's out of sync with life.

He doesn't feel thirty—or the way he thinks he's supposed to feel. He always thought people who were thirty were grown up, but now he knows he was wrong. He feels like a kid just starting out, only a few feet from his mama and daddy's door, close enough still that he can turn and say something to them, and they might tell him what the world's like, so he'll know and be prepared.

He only recently cried for the first time over the deaths of his mama and daddy, although his daddy has been gone six years and his mama twelve.

He woke up in the middle of the night in the old farmhouse he rents, and he thought for a few seconds he was in his parents' house. He heard a clatter in the kitchen and called, "Mama?" then instantly knew where he was, and Crystal came to the bedroom door and said, "I'm sorry. I dropped a pot." He lay back and closed his eyes. After all those years he only then truly realized he would never see his parents again. He had been in other parts of the country when each of them died and never saw them dead. Their markers in the cemetery were never quite convincing. A part of him always expected to run into them someday, somewhere.

Sometimes Lon wonders what life would be like if he'd become a major-league baseball player the way everyone expected. He doesn't imagine expensive houses or cars much, because he never sees athletes' houses or cars on TV. What he sees is how the stars behave in interviews and how interviewers respond to them. He makes up short speeches and answers to questions he might be asked about his values and interests. "My heroes have always been my daddy, because he was an honest, hardworking man, and Bob Hope, because he makes people laugh and forget their problems, and he loves his country and . . ." He can't say Pete Rose, not after Pete's gambling scandals and getting kicked out of baseball, although Lon thinks Rose was framed. "And Johnny Bench, because he always hustled." But Rose was called Charlie Hustle. "And Johnny Bench because he always gave two hundred percent and projected a positive image of the game." Yes. Lon would tell kids to say no to drugs, to study hard and finish high school, to be good sports, to wear condoms. . . . Maybe not the last part. He would say they should wait till they're married to have sex. "Wait till you're sure you've found that one person meant for you," he'd say. And he imagines Pamela by his side in the interview. Then for some reason the memory of a nude dancer with a shaved pussy flashes in his head. Her name was Reba.

# Five

Since the summer in Raleigh, he's been a dishwasher, sold ice cream, sold encyclopedias, clerked in a liquor store, and managed an apartment building. For three years he thought off and on about becoming a real estate agent. Then he studied for two years for the exam before he got up the nerve to take it. He was scared to death he'd fail. He had nightmares about striking out and dropping balls and about taking the real estate exam with a pen that wouldn't write.

He kept telling himself he *had* to be smarter than that greasy agent who sold his daddy's farm five years ago.

His daddy's farm was sold to a motorcycle gang that wanted it for weekend meetings and summer conferences when members from all over the Midwest got together. The bikers called themselves a club, but they all wore chains and leather jackets, so Lon couldn't help thinking of them as a gang. They all had tattoos, even the women, who looked mean and hard. A fat, ugly one had a tattoo on her meaty biceps saying "Lick me." Lon tries to avoid driving by the farm he grew up on. He hates seeing motorcycles parked around the house and pit bulls chained to the trees. He hates to think what the bikers have done to the inside of his mama's house. Probably turned it into a drug lab.

And he feels so stupid for selling the farm because now here he is renting one. He used to think farms were good only for farming. But he rented the place he now has with a plan in mind. When he has some money, he'll buy the farm, then divide it up into five-acre lots and build log cabins on the lots or set up double-wide mobile homes that don't even look much like mobile homes, and he'll call the properties farmettes and advertise in the Cincinnati and Columbus and Huntington papers and maybe in *Country Living* magazine. The problem, though, is that his entire income for last year was seven thousand dollars, and so far this year he hasn't made a dime.

He knows he should get rid of his Corvette, maybe get some money out of it in addition to trading it for a sedan. Other agents tell him the Vette is the stupidest car he could have, and he always grins and nods but really wants to punch them. He bought it five years ago with the money he got for his parents' farm. It's red, like the one the owner of the Cincinnati Reds gave Pete Rose when he broke Ty Cobb's record for most career hits.

At first the Corvette was like having a new woman. In the parking lot of the Pizza Hut in Peebles, high school kids would gather around him and his car. Girls would gaze at their reflections in the polished hood and stick their heads through the passenger's window and say, "Can I smell your car? I love that smell." The boys made low whistling sounds through their teeth. Lon wore sunglasses and tried not to smile; he wanted to look merely "cool," and after he'd answered questions about the engine and stereo, he'd ask the boys whether any of them played baseball. He'd tell them he had hit .436 in high school, was Most Valuable Player three years in a row. He'd lower his voice and put his hand up to the side of his mouth and tell them he'd fucked all five of West Union High School's cheer-leaders. But almost none of the kids had ever heard of him.

For a few months after he first got the Corvette, he drove past Pamela's house several times a week, hoping she'd see him. One day, finally, she was on her porch, huge with Bobby's baby but still pretty, and Lon slowed down, almost stopped, and he grinned at her, but she just gave him a look of disgust, as if he'd brought some gaudy whore around to try to make her feel bad.

Some of his passion for the car wore off after a while, but he feels comfortable with it, still loves it. It is part of him. Selling it would be like selling his arm or his leg or his dick.

One reason he's glad he moved out of his apartment in West Union and rented the farm is that he can park his Corvette in the barn. He worried about it whenever there was hail or snow, and he was always looking out his apartment window and seeing people sitting on it or parking so close, they knocked their doors against his.

There were actually several reasons for wanting to get out of the apartment. He was the manager of the place and had to hassle people about their rents and fix their backed-up toilets. A couple of months before he moved out, he rented a unit right over his head to a couple of sixteen-year-olds who liked to play their stereo—Janet Jackson and Paula Abdul mostly—

full blast at all hours. They didn't care or it didn't occur to them that they lived right upstairs above the manager. The girl's stomach was big as a Buick. She'd sit in the parking lot in a lawn chair trying to get a tan on her fat legs while she read a *Tiger Beat* magazine propped on her belly. Sometimes she chewed tobacco.

One night she locked the boy out, and he stood at Lon's door with tears streaming down his cheeks and snot hanging from his nose and asked to use Lon's phone.

Lon let him in, and the boy said into the phone, "Mom, she's done it this time. She's done locked me out, and she ain't got no respect for my legal rights as her husband."

One afternoon Lon heard the girl making fun of the boy for flunking his driver's test for the third time. "You couldn't parallel-park if you had a whole dang football field to do it in," Lon heard her braying. He heard the boy smack her and the girl call him a motherfucker.

Then Lon heard things shattering and heavy thumps right above his head.

# Six

Crystal sits at the card table in the center of the bomb shelter, staring at the candles she lit. She has never been in such a quiet place. She doesn't have a watch, but she slept for what felt like a long time.

One thing is for sure: She doesn't want to leave the shelter yet—not until she has some idea of what to do with her life.

The candles cast eerie shadows, but she's been watching them long enough now that they don't bother her. Last month when Lon showed her this place, he said, "Don't you think it's kind of romantic down here? It would be up to *us* to repopulate the world." She told him she thought it was creepy.

He shut the hatch, lit two candles, turned off the flashlight, and said, "See?"

"It's still not romantic, Lon. It's a bomb shelter. You'd come down here and know that outside everybody was dying."

"But we'd be like Adam and Eve."

"What are you saying?"

"I'm sayin' take your clothes off."

She pushed him away and turned toward a shelf lined with jugs of water. "You saying you want a baby?"

"Did I say that?"

"You're talking about repopulating the world."

He took hold of her shoulders and pulled her close. He brushed her hair away from her neck and kissed her, sliding his tongue up to her ear. "No, girl. This is just an air-raid *drill*." Then he laughed.

She gazes at the unwavering flames of the candles. It's not as cold down here as it is outside, but she'd like to warm up the shelter. She has on a sweater, buttoned to the neck.

She lights another candle. Don't some people light candles for the dead? And she thinks of Buck's accident, how he almost bled to death before stumbling across that soybean field he was harvesting, out onto the road, which another farmer's wife just happened to be driving down on her way into West Union. What a sight that poor woman must have seen: Buck crazed and bloody—his right hand gone, chopped up and digested by the huge, green combine. But she drove him to the hospital, something Crystal is not sure she could have done. She's glad Buck headed for the road instead of trying to make it to the house. She probably would have fainted and then awakened with his dead body beside her.

In the hospital Buck said the combine hadn't been working right, was getting jammed up, and he was trying to fix it when all of a sudden he felt a jolt. It took his brain a good minute, he said, to accept the fact that the combine had torn his hand off; then he looked in the sky and saw the face of Jesus hovering there, and he thought for sure he'd never see Crystal again.

She has a vision of herself as a respectable widow (instead of a "selfish tramp") being consoled by a crowd of people at the Dunn Funeral home, the most impressive house in Adams County.

She wonders whether Buck's parents would have let her keep the farm if he had died. They gave him their farm when they decided to retire to Atlanta, where Buck's brother works as an architect. She can't imagine why they wouldn't let her keep it. Of course she'd want to sell it after a while and move to a town where interesting things were going on.

*Selfish tramp.*

She lights another candle, imagining Buck riding in that woman's car, slumped forward in the passenger's seat, his eyelids fluttering, his white teeth bared, holding his fresh stump between his legs, blood spreading across the floor mat.

Crystal snatches up an old black-and-white photograph from the card table and glares at it, trying to distract herself away from that horrible image of Buck. In the picture there's a somber-looking man in a dark suit—the farmer who built this shelter, Crystal guesses. The hair around his ears is shaved (whitewalls, her dad calls them). Next to the man is a plain, stout woman and two stout little girls. They're standing in front of a pickup truck with shiny, round fenders and a running board. Maybe they've been to church. Even the little girls look somber, as though they've been sitting on hard pews and hearing about hell.

"Jesus' face was in the sky," Buck said the first time she was allowed to visit him in the hospital in Cincinnati, where he'd been transported by helicopter. Since then he hasn't mentioned seeing Jesus, and Crystal wonders whether he still believes it.

The woman in the photo has an ugly fifties hairdo that reminds Crystal of Beaver Cleaver's mom, but the little girls, despite the serious expressions, are cute, and a familiar ache glows in her chest.

Last winter, a year ago, she delivered a stillborn baby girl. The doctors didn't know what went wrong. They told her there was no reason, but she wouldn't believe that. She tried to figure out on her own what had gone wrong, but the medical books in the West Union Free Public Library didn't help much. They contradicted each other, and she couldn't understand what some words meant, even after she looked them up in a dictionary. One moldy old book talked about attaching leeches to pregnant women's bellies. Maybe there really was no reason—or at least one that could be understood—and that seemed more horrible than anything else she could have discovered.

After waiting a couple of months she and Buck started trying to get pregnant again, but then Buck had his accident.

Ever since she was little, despite whatever else she wanted out of life (like being Miss U.S.A. and a soap-opera star), she has wanted a baby. Now she doesn't know whether she wants to have Lon's baby or Buck's baby.

The first few months of her marriage she had a recurring dream about getting off a school bus in front of Buck's farm and walking into a house full of girl babies that looked like her and boy babies that looked like Buck, a dozen of each. Two months ago she was certain she wanted to have a baby with a guy named Doc, but Doc turned out to be a jerk.

# Seven

**B**uck is venturing out onto the gravel roads around his farm today. There are a lot of hills and curves, and he stays in second gear, thinks he might wait until tomorrow to try shifting. Driving is one of the things he has to learn to do a new way since he lost his right hand.

It would be easier to have power steering and an automatic transmission, but Buck would like at least a few things to be the same as always. Getting a different truck, even if he could afford it, would be giving in to—letting himself be controlled by—that empty space at the end of his wrist.

A tractor pulling a hay wagon surprises him on a curve, and he stomps on the brake and stalls. The tractor moves on, and Buck slaps the gear shift into neutral and reaches awkwardly across his chest to turn the ignition key with his left hand.

A couple of days ago he just drove circles around the barn, practicing steering and staying in first gear. After a while first gear seemed too slow and boring, so he tried starting out in second, fighting the truck's desire to stall out. In the confines of the barnyard second gear was fast. The chickens squawked, ran into each other, and took flight. A couple bounced off the windshield. When he stopped, he sat for a moment and watched the glistening dust settle. His left arm and shoulder ached, and although the temperature was around forty, he was sweaty and his flannel shirt clung to his back.

He slid out of the pickup, a beat-up twenty-five-year-old Ford his dad bought the year Buck was born, and stared down at two dirty, stupid-looking, dead chickens on the ground. He picked them up by their claws and walked down the hill behind the barn toward the big ditch where his family has always dumped their garbage. When he got about twenty feet from the edge, he heaved the chickens. On their short flight their heads flopped back and forth in a silly way. They fell short of the ditch. Buck swore. He left them, went up to his empty house, and put a turkey potpie in the oven for his supper.

Yesterday he drove up and down his long, rutted driveway. He wanted to practice shifting gears before going out onto the road where people might catch him making a fool of himself. He bumped the gear-shift lever with his stump. Jolting along at thirty, the transmission whining, he kept knocking it into first gear when he needed third. Rocks scraped the bottom of the truck; gravel flew up through the rusted-out floorboards.

Reverse was almost impossible. He had to reach across

himself and pull up the lever with his left hand and jerk it into the lower right-hand corner.

Going up and down the driveway, he twice ran into the muddy corn field that preceded the house's front yard, where years ago his mother arranged half a dozen pink plastic flamingos in flower beds. The flower beds got choked by weeds after she and Buck's dad moved to Atlanta.

Trying to shift into fourth, going nearly fifty down the driveway toward the house, Buck hit a large rut, lost his grip on the steering wheel, and suddenly found himself on the passenger's side of the cab, the steering wheel shimmying crazily—as if the truck were being driven by an insane phantom. The truck plowed up the front yard. There were sounds like bones crunching. Then a pink flamingo popped up through the floorboard. Just before the truck stalled, Buck thought he was going to crash and die, was certain he was about to see Jesus again.

# Eight

Now, on a stretch of straight road, Buck tries to bump the lever into third, but he ends up in neutral and coasts along until he manages to get back into second. When he comes to another straight stretch, he gets third gear, but when he tries fourth, he slips into second. The old Ford shudders, and Buck hits his chin on the top of the steering wheel. He decides to stay in second for a while, feeling a bump swell up on his chin.

An artificial hand or even a hook might be a big help, but Crystal was grossed out by the idea, and although she's living with another man now, he's hoping she'll come back.

About a week before she left, he was looking at a catalog he'd gotten in the mail from Pate's Prostheses, and he called to her from his chair in the living room: "I can start doin' some work, if I get me one of these things."

"What things?" She was at the table in the kitchen, fooling with a pile of photographs.

From where he sat, he could see her. She was framed by the kitchen doorway. He had the TV on to watch "The Young and the Restless," one of his favorite soap operas. He'd started watching soap operas in the hospital and kept all the nurses updated. He liked all the good-looking women on the shows. On "The Days of Our Lives," the women were all after a guy who wore an eye patch. One of the things that fascinated Buck was how characters who were supposed to be dead often turned out not to be. Even if you saw a dead body, it would usually turn out to be some long-lost twin who just happened to get into town the day the murderer struck or the accident occurred. Sometimes actors quit for good, but their characters were too important to kill off, so they'd get mutilated, then restored. They'd have no scars; they would lose nothing. They only looked different.

But the catalog had come in the mail, and Buck wasn't paying attention to the TV. Apparently Crystal was listening in the kitchen because a few minutes before he called to her, she had said, "He's just using her. She's gonna get burned by him for sure. You get him out of those fancy clothes and he probably isn't much to look at anyway." Buck had looked up from his catalog. A commercial was coming on, and he didn't have the slightest idea what she was talking about.

Now he said, "One of these things in this book. A hand."

"A what?"

He watched her. She didn't look up from her pictures. "One of these mechanical hands," he said. "Or something cheaper, like a hook."

The word *hook* seemed to get her attention. She looked up. Her mouth dropped open. She held a photograph in her fingers. "Buck, you hear me now. I don't ever want to hear you say something like that again. Are you trying to turn my stomach?" She laid the photograph down.

"But . . ." He looked down at the catalog on his lap. Smiling models showed off artificial hands and arms and legs. Under the picture of a woman in a long formal dress dancing with a man in a white tuxedo a caption said, "You can even dance!" Buck looked up and said, "I could—"

"I don't want to hear about hooks. God!"

He closed the catalog. On the cover were a young couple on bicycles, a good-looking man with a mechanical leg and a sexy girl in shorts and a halter top. The girl wasn't missing any limbs. She had long blond hair and a slim build, except for big, pointy breasts. She looked a lot like Crystal. Crystal could be a model, Buck thought. She'd been Miss Pumpkin Festival 1987 and Miss Adams County 1988.

Secretly and guiltily Buck was glad Crystal hadn't done well in the Miss Ohio beauty pageant, although he was amazed she didn't win. When he had met her at church a few months before the Miss Ohio competition, he thought she looked like a girl on a beer commercial—she was *that* beautiful. He hadn't gone to church in years, but his parents were going to their last Christmas service before moving to Atlanta for the rest of their lives, and they talked Buck into going with them. The preacher stood up front and addressed each person individually. He said, "May God bless you this Christmas." Then he said something nice about everyone: "Harold there has a wonderful sense of humor. If you don't know him, you should." There were about a hundred people, and the preacher had to give a lot of them the same label. Several women were "won-

derful mothers," including Buck's; men were "generous con-
tributors to the church" or "good fathers" or "good neighbors";
Buck was a "fine young farmer and devoted son"; young boys
were "scholars" or "athletes"; the girls were "pious virgins" (a
statement that made a lot of girls squirm) or "great beauties,"
a lie when applied to most of them but no exaggeration in
Crystal's case. Buck remembered her name, looked her parents up in the phone book, and called her Christmas night.

In Columbus the following spring Crystal didn't make
even the semifinals of the Miss Ohio pageant. But she put on
a good show for everybody afterward, smiling and congratulat-
ing the winner and the first runner-up, hugging all the girls
she'd pretended to make friends with in their weekend together. Then in the car with Buck she stopped acting. "Don't
start driving yet," she said. "I just want to sit here a minute."

She stared at the civic center the contest had been held
in. Buck had the motor running and the windshield wipers going. A storm had come up suddenly, and gusts rocked the car.
They had driven her Volkswagen Bug so that she could ride
with him but not arrive at the contest in a pickup truck. The
parking lot was empty except for them, and it crossed Buck's
mind that they could make out a little, but he was already
starting to see she wasn't in a good mood, wasn't the gracious
loser she had pretended to be.

"I'm almost glad I didn't win," she said. "All those girls
are catty as can be. Half of them wear colored contact lenses
and dye their hair, and that Melissa from Dayton hasn't got the
boobs God gave her, I'm almost certain."

"Oh, honey," Buck said, and put his arm around her.

She shrugged his arm off. "I know I can't act."

"Huh?"

"Act. You know. Act. I mean, I never got any big parts in

the school plays—the brainy girls always get those. But those women on soap operas can't act either. They're just pretty women all made up to look real stunning. I guess I can forget about that."

"I think you're the most beautiful girl in the world."

"Don't get corny on me, okay? Besides, I know it's not true. I don't even rank in the top ten in Ohio."

Soft, in a solemn tone, Buck said, "I love you, Crystal. I mean that."

"You know sometimes I wish I didn't live in a state where the competition was so tough. I wish I lived in Idaho or someplace."

"Will you—"

"Then again maybe I ought to just be glad I don't live in Texas."

"Will you marry me?"

"Every girl you see on TV is from Texas."

"I'm askin' you to marry me."

"We're talking about *me* now."

"What?"

She was looking off at a corner of the civic center or at a lamppost or at the rain. Maybe, he thought, she was looking at something he couldn't see.

"Big bump," she said quietly.

"What?"

"Big bump. On her nose."

"Who?"

"Nobody."

He sighed.

"Fucking smile."

"Listen," Buck said. He shut off the windshield wipers because they were squeaking. "In a month you're gonna graduate high school. And I got my own farm, and I love you. So you wanta get married?"

She looked at him out of the corner of her eye, then back out the window. Now he was sure she must be looking at something he couldn't see. A gust of wind rocked the car.

She muttered something he couldn't hear. He watched her take a deep breath, and she transformed. When she turned to him, her face had changed, was glowing, and she threw her arms around him and said, "I'll make you happy, Buck."

Before Buck lost his hand, Crystal often went around the house in flimsy, short nightgowns and T-shirts without a bra underneath. But after his accident she started wearing long, heavy robes. The day he got the catalog from Pate's Prostheses, she sat looking at photographs, wearing baggy denim overalls.

He got out of his armchair and headed toward the kitchen. That morning she had been gone when he woke up. He had looked in his brother's old bedroom for her, but she'd already made up the bed. A half hour later she came home with two photo albums. "I've got a bunch of pictures in envelopes I want to straighten out and put in these books," she said.

She didn't look up when he entered the kitchen. Snapshots were arranged on the table in long, straight rows and apparently in chronological order. The first one on the top row showed her as a baby barely old enough to sit up, wearing a frilly pink dress. Her hair was curly then. On the bottom row were several pictures she'd cut in half. Buck had known other girls who'd done that to photographs they'd had taken with boys they didn't like anymore. In two of Crystal's pictures there were disembodied hands on her shoulder. In another she was holding a disembodied hand in her own. In one she wore a glittering crown and her homecoming formal; a hand that came from nowhere was on her waist.

"Is that Scott Wilder's hand?" he asked.

"Yeah. He was Homecoming King, but he was also an egomaniac, and I'm sorry I wasted six months of my life on him."

Buck nodded. He remembered what an asshole Wilder was. She had started dating Buck before she broke up with Wilder. She'd tell Wilder lies about being sick or going out with her girlfriends or having to visit her grandmother, and she and Buck would drive forty miles to Portsmouth to see a movie or eat at Dairy Queen or park behind Portsmouth Junior High School. The next night she'd be out with Wilder.

Once, Buck passed them on Main Street in West Union. Crystal was sitting close to Wilder in his Mustang. Buck turned his truck around and followed them twelve miles to Peebles, where high school kids always went to eat. They parked at McDonald's and went inside. Buck parked on the street, then got out. He looked around as he walked toward the Mustang. He circled it once, looking for flaws, scratches or bubbles in the paint job. He didn't find any. Standing at the rear of the car, he took a deep breath, then kicked out the taillights.

Somehow Wilder found out who did it, and two days later Buck found his mailbox smashed and the mailbox post sawed up into stubby logs, evidently with a chain saw. At three in the morning Buck went into West Union to Wilder's house, armed with a double-blade ax. Wilder's parents had just a little mailbox attached to the house next to the front door, so Buck looked around and decided to chop up a garden hose somebody had left strung across the front yard. Then he chopped down a young pear tree before lights came on in the house.

Looking at the rows of snapshots on the kitchen table,

Buck said, "Wilder was a pussy." Buck had expected the war between him and Wilder to go on, but it hadn't. "I wish he had come around with that chain saw of his again. I'd of showed him the Ohio Chain Saw Massacre." But Buck was actually relieved he hadn't. A week after Crystal finally broke up with him, Buck saw Wilder in his Mustang with a red-headed pom-pom girl.

Leaning toward Crystal, Buck made a noise like a chain saw, trying to be entertaining.

"Will you stop it."

Buck found a picture of himself: sitting on his tractor, a big grin on his face, his Massey-Ferguson cap pushed back on his head, his hands huge on the steering wheel. "This is nice," he said. "The story of your life in pictures." Then he made the mistake of patting the back of her shoulder with his stump, and she jumped up, mumbling something.

"What?" he asked.

She shook her head on her way to the sink full of dirty cups and silverware. The garbage can was full of potpie and TV-dinner containers. She reached for the spigot, then stopped and reached up to a cabinet and took down a glass.

"I like pictures," she said. "They make things stand still." She opened the refrigerator and poured a Coke from a plastic two-liter bottle. She stood drinking the Coke with the refrigerator door open. The refrigerator's motor kicked on, hummed.

When she tipped her head back to drink, Buck thought how nice her long, thick hair was.

# Nine

Crystal is lying on a cot. On the wall above her head is a Dunn Funeral Home calendar, a picture of the stately house and grounds, a perfect blue sky above it all. What would her life be like now if her baby had not died? Died for no apparent reason, the doctors said. If Buck had not had his accident? A freak accident, everybody said.

On the opposite wall are shelves of canned juices, beans, and fruit cocktail. The cans, Lon told her, are only a year or two old. The farmer, after his daughters grew up and moved away and his wife died, stayed prepared, right up to the end. On another wall there's a dart board.

Crystal gets up and goes over to a shelf on which a Bible and some darts lie, and she starts tossing the darts at the dart board. One hits the concrete wall and bounces back at her.

*Selfish tramp.*

What does her mother know. The silly woman has had a perfectly boring, normal life. Or maybe not normal at all. She never dated anyone except Crystal's dad, then married him when she was seventeen, and has always been content. Yes, content, she said when Crystal was fifteen and wanted to know everything her mother could tell her about love; always content at least, if not always blissful. By the time she was fifteen, Crystal's romantic notions about love had become tainted, and she was confused. Thoughts of love conjured up a collage of strange images—a frilly white dress and a hairy hand, a night sky full of stars and a guy's pale butt, a bouquet of flowers and blood on her thighs. Love seemed both beautiful and ugly, serious and sick.

What does her mother know.

But Crystal envies her mother, who appears to love Crystal's dad in some old-fashioned way. Antique love, Crystal thinks. Waltons love.

She has caught her parents kissing passionately in front of the kitchen sink—bliss—the hot water running, the sink full of dirty dishes. Kissing in full view of dried egg yolks and bacon grease.

Her mother brings Dad Cokes while he watches ball games, and he doesn't even ask her to. She probably doesn't even notice, or at least doesn't care, how nice a lot of football players' butts are.

A dart sticks close to the bull's-eye. Butts. Now she's thinking of Doc. She decides to pretend that the bull's-eye is Doc's heart.

After Buck came home from the hospital, she started working at Kmart because they needed the money, and besides, she wanted to get out of the house, away from Buck and

his stump. One day her second week at work she was ringing
up a dozen Christmas ornaments when she glanced over to the
bank of entrance doors and caught Doc staring at her. He was
standing next to the Salvation Army Santa Claus, who was
smoking a cigarette and smirking and talking loudly: "They
think they can tell me what to do. Huh! They don't know shit.
I'll fix their wagon." Doc was nodding, but he clearly had his
attention focused on Crystal.

He was tall and thin, in his late twenties, probably two or
three years older than Buck, and had blond hair. His eyebrows
were so light, they were almost invisible. He dressed in three-
piece suits as if he were a big-city executive, and Crystal had
already noticed that customers often mistook him for the manager, even when Doc was standing right next to the manager,
a bald little man who wore bow ties. Doc was the assistant
manager. Chuck "Doc" Smith, his name tag said.

He stared at her and didn't drop his eyes when she caught
him. She reached up and touched all three earrings (tiny fake
diamonds) in her right earlobe, one at a time. It was a nervous
habit she was aware of but couldn't help. She bagged the
Christmas ornaments, said, "Thank you for shopping at
Kmart" (the manager had told her she could be fired for not
saying that), then glanced at Doc again. This time he smiled.
She said hello to her next customer. Santa rang his bell. She
looked again, and Doc winked at her.

The week before, a tall, gawky woman had come into the
stockroom where the employees took their breaks and said to
Crystal, who was sitting at a card table and eating a peanut-
butter-and-jelly sandwich, "Would you ever pose in the nude?"

"What?"

"I just heard this girl say some farmers are going to print
a calendar showing nude women driving tractors and pitching

hay. Stuff like that. Digging fence-post holes. And they'll use the money they make to help farmers in trouble pay off loans." She paused. "I'm sorry. You don't know me, do you? I'm Anita. I work in Home Improvement." She looked at Crystal's sandwich. "So you in high school or something?"

Crystal looked at her sandwich, too, and felt foolish. Then she found herself telling the woman all about Buck's accident and how they didn't have much money.

Anita said, "I bet posing nude pays a lot better than Kmart. Hell, I'd do it, but who's going to ask me? Listen, Crystal, if you need anything, let me know. Kmart's the pits."

Anita seemed weird, but the other girls weren't friendly. They were all chubby and had bad complexions. Her second day at work Crystal walked into the stockroom when three girls were talking about her—at least she was almost sure they were. She had heard the word *princess* said in a nasty tone, and as soon as the girls saw her, they shut up. Crystal smiled at them. One girl rolled her eyes at another, and they all left, leaving Crystal alone with the phony smile frozen on her face.

The day Crystal caught Doc staring at her, she asked Anita why he was called Doc. She said he was a medical-school dropout. Anita sucked her cigarette and then blew out the smoke very dramatically. Crystal watched it drift toward the exposed beams of the stockroom's ceiling. "He couldn't stand seeing little kids dying all the time or something."

Crystal asked whether Doc was married, and Anita's eyes lit up. Crystal was struck by how much she looked like Big Bird on "Sesame Street." She was over six feet and had a big frizzy hairdo, kind of a blond Afro. "Doc's a stud, don't you think?" Anita said.

"He's all right." Crystal stared at a stack of boxes stamped FRAGILE and touched her earrings.

"He's married, but let me tell you—his wife came in one time, and somebody pointed her out to me, and I about died. She's real short, about three feet—"

"Three feet?"

"Well, maybe I'm exaggerating. But not much. And she's kind of fat. Not real fat, but she could stand to drop a few pounds. She's about a negative two on a scale of ten compared with you."

"They got any kids?"

"No. You ever see Sally Field when she was the flying nun on TV? She used to look a little chubby. Had a real round face?"

"I don't think so."

"Well, his wife looks like that."

"Like a flying nun?"

"It was an old TV show." Crystal guessed Anita was in her thirties. She had crinkles around her eyes. "You want me to talk to him for you?" Anita asked.

"No! I mean, what for?"

"You know the motto. 'Kmart is the shopping place.' "

That night, in Buck's brother's old room, Crystal dreamed about Doc. He stood in a dark-blue three-piece suit at the bank of entrance doors at Kmart and was ringing a brass bell as though he had taken the place of the Salvation Army Santa Claus. He smiled and nodded at people who dropped coins into his pot. At his side, so short her head barely cleared his knees, was a fat nun in a black habit. Then the nun lifted her arms and she looked like a bat.

Over the next few days Doc started saying hi to Crystal

every time he walked past her checkout station, and he spent a lot of time explaining to her the options she had concerning her work schedule. He didn't seem to do that with anyone else.

At home she said, "I really like working, Buck. I can work all the overtime I want, so I think I will."

"You do what you want," Buck muttered. "God knows I can't stop you."

Buck sat sullen in front of the TV. Since his accident he'd gotten into the habit of watching daytime soap operas. Crystal liked soap operas herself, but she thought something was wrong with a man who did. "I don't know," she said to Anita one day at work. "It's like a woman wanting to play football or something, I guess. Any day now I expect him to be reading Harlequin romances."

Buck sat in a big, worn-out armchair that used to be his father's. The right armrest had several small holes from cigarette burns. Buck had stopped smoking when he was twenty, but started again after losing his hand, and now he was putting burns in the left armrest. He seldom got out of the chair, but whenever she was in the living room, Crystal kept on the move, flitting from one spot to another, picking up a farmer's magazine from the coffee table and putting it down on the end table, moving an empty candle holder from the fireplace mantel to the old pedal sewing machine, dragging the rocking chair from one corner to another (leaving scratches on the hardwood floor); she was constantly rearranging the living room because it never looked right anymore. Also, she wanted to be on her toes, a difficult target—in case Buck came out of his chair at her and tried to touch her with his stump.

*Selfish tramp.*

*But, Mama,* she wants to say, *didn't you teach me to put*

*myself first? When I was little, you entered me in those beauty contests for children and told me to cut the other kids' throats with my smile.*

She flings another dart and completely misses the board. It glances off the wall. On the floor, in the shadows, its feathers mussed, the dart looks like a small, dead bird.

She looks at the cans of food, shakes her head. She lies down on the cot, stretches, closes her eyes, and hopes for a sweet, dreamless nothingness.

# Ten

Lon goes into the bathroom and examines himself in the mirror. He splashes cold water on his face, the pipes groaning and screeching when he turns the spigot. There are three long scratches on his left cheek.

Back at the front window he looks at the plastic flags flapping in the wind, wondering what made him think he could be a real estate agent.

Then a Honda Civic pulls into the driveway, and a couple about Lon's age get out. Lon pats the cowlick on the crown of his head as he stands in the doorway, smiling. When they get close, he says, "Howdy. Good afternoon. I'm Lon Peterson. Valley Realty." He shakes hands with the man and gives the woman his card. The man introduces himself and his wife, but Lon is not good at catching people's names; he doesn't really hear them because his mind rushes through an analysis of their appearances and what kind of approach he should take with them.

The wife stares at Lon's face. She opens her mouth to speak but pauses, and Lon thinks she's going to ask him about his scratches; then she asks, "What's the price?"

"It's been reduced for a quick sale. Thirty-two five."

Lon steps aside so that they can come in, and the woman gingerly touches a place where the plaster is crumbling.

The house belonged to an old woman who died last year. Her nephew sold the furniture to antique dealers and now wants whatever he can get for the house without doing any repairs.

"You want some punch?" Lon asks. He bought three cans of Hawaiian Punch and some paper cups. In the newspaper he advertised "refreshments served."

"No, thank you," the woman says.

She and her husband are both wearing wool sweaters and designer jeans. Lon's guess is they're city people out on a Sunday drive. They probably own a condo in Cincinnati but like to look at old houses. "You know, Adams County's got the lowest real estate prices in the state," he tells them.

Lon stays in the living room while they go through the house. They whisper. The man laughs once. When they come back to the front door, Lon tells them the furnace is only five years old, the roof eight; the septic tank has never backed up, at least not as far as anybody can recall.

When they drive off, Lon watches them. They don't look back.

# Eleven

L on sits down on the edge of the bathtub, drinking from the quart bottle of Hudepohl beer he's had hidden in the toilet tank. Once, recently, he found himself opening a beer for breakfast and worried about his drinking as he sat at his kitchen table and went through a six-pack.

He decided he couldn't have a problem because his daddy never had a problem. His daddy drank like a fish when he had time, in the winter when there was nothing to do but feed the animals. But when spring came, he stopped and worked through the summer and fall and didn't touch a drop of alcohol until the fields were nothing but stubble.

Before Lon was old enough to go to school, his daddy would take him into Mount Orab most winter days to a bar that opened at eight in the morning. That was when his mama still taught third grade at the elementary school in West Union; Daddy had to baby-sit him. In the bar each morning four or five other people would be there. They'd say, "Cute kid," to Lon's daddy. Lon always sat on a stool, feeling way up off the ground, drinking Cokes served in little shot glasses and staring at himself in the mirror behind the bar. Daddy sat beside him, quiet, drinking whiskey, or he'd sit in a booth in back with two or three other men. They'd laugh sometimes; sometimes their voices were angry. But Lon never listened to their words.

The place had barely any light. The walls were covered with dark imitation-wood paneling. It was cold, and Lon could hear the winter wind howling.

Every three weeks or so his daddy took him to the barbershop next door and left him there with an old man whose hands shook. The old barber would crank the chair up, crank it and crank it, and swing it around to the window so Lon could see outside. A hardware store and Scarlet's Café were across the street. Scarlet's had a huge front window, and Lon often saw fat Scarlet standing in the middle of the empty café in her waitress's uniform, holding a broom and smoking a cigarette and gazing out at the street. It always seemed to be snowing or raining. The barber didn't talk. He breathed hard and nipped Lon's ears with his scissors.

Then Lon would go back to the bar and stare at himself in the mirror while he sipped a Coke from a shot glass, his hair short and ragged, his ears stinging. His daddy would come over to him and put his arm around him and breathe his whiskey breath into Lon's face. "You didn't want them ears anyway, did ya?" His daddy would kiss his head, and Lon felt embarrassed but warmer; and holding out his empty shot glass, Lon would say loudly to the bartender, "Hit me again, Sammy."

Sometimes his daddy took him to the woods. They'd follow a trail up and down several hills until they got to a clearing where men were gathered around a still, some standing, others sitting with their backs against trees, all of them drinking moonshine out of mason jars. A gray-haired black man named Oscar had a lopsided, scarred-up baseball he and Lon tossed back and forth, until the cold got to Lon's fingers and he lost all his feeling in them. Lon liked the clearing in the woods better than he did the bar. Then one day the old black man wasn't there and was never there again. Daddy said he didn't know where the colored man was, speculated that maybe Oscar inherited a lot of money and moved away. Years later, when Lon was in high school and talking one day about his dreams of being a professional baseball player, Daddy asked him whether he remembered the old colored man who taught him how to throw and catch, and Lon said he did. Then Daddy told him the truth, that Oscar had died from drinking turpentine.

Sitting on the edge of the bathtub, Lon leans back his head and takes a long drink with his eyes closed and remembers a dream he had last night. His mama was cranking the siren on his front porch, the fat of her arms flapping, while his daddy ran around gathering up and holding like a bundle of wiggling fur coats all of Lon's childhood pets, several cats and dogs; Lon saw himself running down the road, then the driveway, frantic to get his mama and daddy to the bomb shelter before it was too late; and he saw Crystal and Pamela and Kim and Gina and Reba—a whole string of women dropping down into the shelter; and the scream and screeches of the siren sounded like the words *Seek shelter! Seek shelter!*

Now he remembers that he also dreamed he made love to

Pamela on a cot in the bomb shelter while Crystal stood watching and saying, "I love you, Lon. Do you hear me?"

He wonders whether Crystal will be out of the shelter when he gets home.

# Twelve

A cherry-looking '69 Chevy pulls in the driveway. A guy by himself gets out, wearing jeans and a denim jacket over a T-shirt. Guys without their wives are a waste of time. Wives are the ones who pick out houses. Still, Lon smiles, shakes his hand, and catches his first name: Jake. The first thing he asks Lon is how much the place is. Nobody with a name like Jake has money.

Lon follows him around. Jake never once looks at him. He talks to floors, ceilings, walls, windowpanes, asking about financing options.

"You got a family, Jake?"

"A wife and little girl."

"You renting now?"

"Not really."

"Not really?" Lon is too tired for this. "You want to give

me some information so I can figure out what you can afford. There's lots of houses on the market. Some cheaper than this. Where you work, Jake?"

"Thanks for your time, mister."

And the guy strides out, doesn't look back. As soon as he's laid rubber down the street, an old Ford Falcon pulls up. More losers, Lon's sure. The rear quarter panels of the Falcon are rusted out, and black smoke hangs in the car's wake. It's not the car of people who can get loan approval. A young couple in their early twenties get out and saunter toward the house. The woman is very small and has straight black hair. She has a white dress on, and the man has on jeans and sneakers with a coat and tie. She smiles, points at something, and takes the man's arm. He nods. Then Lon recognizes him as his ex-brother-in-law.

"Well, how are you, Darrell? Long time," Lon says, meeting him on the stoop.

They shake hands warmly. Lon is amazed. He remembers Darrell as a freckle-faced kid who wanted to hang around him and Pamela all the time.

"This is my wife, Suk." Lon sees now that she's foreign, Korean perhaps. She nods, smiles, avoids eye contact. "I just got out of the army," Darrell says.

"I heard you were in."

"So you're sellin' houses, huh?"

"Tryin'. How's your mom?"

"She's okay." Darrell's wife goes into the house. Darrell grins. "What happened to your face?"

"Ah, my cat scratched me."

"What were you tryin' to do to her?"

"Just pet her."

Darrell looks around. Lon sees him furrow his eyebrows

at the tree stumps in the front yard. Still looking at them, he says, "Pamela's a nurse now, you know."

"Oh yeah?"

"Got her LPN at the junior college in Portsmouth."

"Yeah?"

"Well."

"So what you going to do now you're not defending democracy?"

Darrell's face lights up. "I got on as a county deputy."

"Well, congratulations."

"Don't drink and drive."

"Never do."

"Job don't pay a lot. Nothin' like what you real estate agents make, but I think me and Suk can afford a place like this. We've been stayin' with Mom. She can't understand a word Suk says. I'm used to her accent, but Mom can't even tell that she's speakin' English, and she acts nervous all the time. Besides, Suk's got bread bakin' in her oven, if you know what I mean."

"Well, congratulations again. I'd say this is the place for a growing family. You take a look at that backyard. You could field a couple of football teams and a squad of cheerleaders in it."

Lon lets Darrell and his wife look around on their own. "Hey," Darrell calls from the kitchen, "something's burnin' in here."

"You want a TV dinner?" Lon says.

After they leave, Lon retrieves his beer from the toilet tank again. He stands at the living-room window, watching the street and surveying the yard. A strong breeze comes up and flaps the plastic flags, making a racket.

"Hot damn!" Lon says out loud. Darrell said he'd probably call tonight after he and Suk talk it over. Lon tries to figure his commission in his head.

# Thirteen

Lon starts locking up the house at three because he knows the whole county will be at the parade this afternoon. Already he hears a bass drum beating, then some snare drums—crazy sounds from the kids in the West Union High School marching band pretending to be rock stars. The band is down in the school parking lot getting ready for the parade. A loud splat from a tuba joins in, then a couple of shrill notes from a trumpet. The noise stops suddenly. The band director is probably giving them hell for screwing around.

Tubbs is the band director's name. He was around back when Lon went to West Union High. Lon always thought he looked like a fag—short, soft, pale—but in eleventh grade Pamela told Lon that Tubbs put his hand on her butt in his office while he was giving her some private instruction on the clarinet. When Pamela jumped away, Tubbs said he was just trying to help her hit the high notes. Lon would have beaten the crap out of Tubbs if Pamela hadn't stopped him. Back then Lon figured he could get away with anything because he was a star athlete. He was more important than a band director.

He walks up to the end of the street where a crowd has gathered, the biggest crowd Lon's ever seen in West Union. People are lined around the town square where the courthouse is. He heard that the parade is going to come the two blocks from the high school, circle the courthouse three times, then go on down to the orphanage at the edge of town so that the kids who live there can shake hands with the mayor (as if any of them gave a shit about the old man) and with Yvonne Strickland, who has come all the way from California.

Farmers in overalls and their fat wives try to make their kids stand still. The kids are all worked up. Old folks have brought lawn chairs and unfolded them on the edge of the sidewalk, but half the crowd has already gotten in front of them, and the old men and women sit with people's butts in their faces.

The parade is the kickoff of the town's bicentennial. The mayor and the merchants hope the economy will be helped by the hoopla.

Lon sees his old buddy Dale and his wife making their way through the crowd toward him. Dale played first base and graduated from West Union High the same year Lon did.

"You see her yet?" Dale says.

"Who?"

"Yvonne."

"No."

"I hear she's real good-lookin'. Better than she used to look."

"Yeah? You better keep your eye on him, Becky." Lon grins at Dale. "Dale's got himself the hots for an old movie star."

"More power to him," Becky says, looking around.

"See, you already got her pissed off at you," Lon says. Dale smiles uneasily.

"I'm gonna go talk to Anita," Becky says.

"She here?" Dale says.

"Yeah, I see her."

"Okay. I'll catch you in a minute."

Lon says, "Just don't let Becky take any beauty tips from that Anita. Man, she's friends with Crystal, and every time she comes around, I get the heebie-jeebies. Always smells like rancid butter or somethin', for one thing."

"You don't know the half of it."

"What you mean?"

"Maybe I'll go into it someday when I'm drunk. How's Crystal?"

Lon hesitates. "She's okay." Then he grins. "Girl never cools off. The government oughta regulate her. I'm afraid it's gonna fall off if I'm not careful."

Dale doesn't seem to be paying attention. He's looking off in the direction that Becky went in. The band has started playing down at the high school.

Lon suddenly feels sad. He and Dale were great buddies in high school, but they don't seem to click anymore. Dale gets into deep moods often these days. He explains his theories for curing America's problems, most of which involve blowing away Communists and camel jockeys and TV preachers and rap singers. Lon liked it better when Dale was obsessed with baseball and pussy.

"Hey, Dale."

"Listen, Lon, I better find Becky."

"Sure. I'll see you."

People lined along the road down toward the high school are cheering. The parade has started. Lon thinks about leaving, but it would take some work fighting the crowd.

Behind the marching band is a red pickup truck with FFA members in the back, looking like the hicks they are. Then come trucks full of football players and basketball players, then a convertible with the cheerleaders. There are some floats built over trailers and pulled by cars. The floats are made out of cardboard and paper and ribbons—a giant pumpkin, a tobacco leaf, an ear of corn. Lon thinks there should be a float representing the moonshine industry.

The frail little mayor, the old man who used to be Lon's daddy's lawyer, rides in a convertible with Miss Adams County 1991, a girl not nearly as pretty as Crystal—or Pamela for that matter.

Behind them, standing in the back of a Cadillac convertible by herself, is Yvonne Strickland.

She's smiling big and waving like crazy. Lon hears people comment on how young she looks. And it's true. She's slimmer and prettier in her forties than she is in her old movies. "Another Jane Fonda," a woman says.

An old man wearing thick glasses that make his eyes huge and insane-looking says, "But this one ain't no commy bitch."

Lon hears people talking about the rumor that her rich husband is thinking of financing a movie that would be shot in Adams County and star Yvonne, her big comeback.

"*Butterflies,*" somebody says. "That's the title of it, I think."

Somebody else says, "I heard it was going to be about vampires."

"Is," says a boy about twelve. "*Vampire Butterflies from Hell.*"

"Don't sound like no *Rain Man.*"

"Probably be better than that thing."

"She's made five movies," the boy says. He recites their titles slowly, his eyes focused on his shoes: "*Satan's Touch, Dogs from Hell, Hogs from Hell, The Demon in My House,* and *Bleeding Walls.*"

"Bleeding Balls?" a toothless man says.

"I ain't seen a one of them movies," says an old lady, "and I'm glad."

Lon watches Yvonne Strickland pass, studies her, thinks about how if he'd been luckier, he'd be in this parade, a famous baseball player come home to do his town a favor. The parade is disappearing around the corner of the courthouse. Lon strains his neck to watch. The last vehicle in the parade is West Union's fire truck, the town's only one. It's so old it has spoke wheels. Stretched the length of the truck is a banner saying "1791–1991." Lon thinks it's strange that it's 1991 and that the world is still familiar in most ways. It seems that by now the world should look the way it does on the "Jetsons" cartoons he watched when he was a kid. Maybe someday it will, but even if much of the world someday lives in the sky and is waited on by robots, people around here will still be living in old frame houses and mobile homes on concrete blocks.

Then he sees Pamela. She's on the other side of the street, struggling with her little boy, who keeps wanting to run out into the road, it looks like. She's bent over, holding on to her son's arm, and he sits down in the gutter and starts kicking her shins. Her hair is limp and falls across her face. She lifts the boy and shakes him, her face red. Her face is broader than it used to be, thicker, paler.

Some big guy comes up from behind her and lifts the kid and puts him on his shoulders. The boy smiles. The kid is five now, Lon calculates. He looks as scrawny and stupid as Bobby did.

Pamela looks up at her son and smiles, her old prettiness coming back, glowing through. People around here age fast, Lon thinks. He remembers his daddy saying you could never tell whether a woman from here was thirty or fifty. If Yvonne Strickland had stayed here, Lon is certain she'd be a hag.

Looking at Pamela, Lon feels a flutter in his chest and an ache in his loins. A dozen years. A dozen years since he last made love to her. He shakes his head, amazed.

## Fourteen

The parade is really depressing for Pamela: Matt is wild;
Yvonne Strickland looks gorgeous (Pamela, for some reason, had hoped she'd be a pig); and Roy shows up.

Afterward Pamela drops Matt off at her mother's house,
for the third time this week, to spend the night. She kisses him
good-bye, knows she'll miss him later the way she always does,
but sighs with relief when she drives away without him.

Matt was born looking like Pamela's dead husband—the
gray slits of eyes, the thin lips, the sharp nose—and it has only
gotten worse each year. In the delivery room, when the nurse
handed Matt to her—a slick, bloody gargoyle—it was as if
Bobby, after all those months during which Pamela felt free
and safe and prayed for the birth of a girl, had found a way to
come back and haunt her.

This morning by the time she got up, Matt had painted the hall outside the bathroom with her makeup and fingernail polish. He, the carpet, and the wall were covered with smears of eye shadow, highlighter, scarlet nail polish, and baby powder. She was so horrified by the sight that she didn't notice at first the strong scent of her favorite perfume.

"Look at what you did!" she yelled. "This stuff costs a lot of money. The carpet is ruined. The wall . . . Look! Look! Look!"

Matt looked, seemed bewildered, then spit at her.

"Okay. Time-out. In your room." She picked him up and tried to carry him to his room, but he kicked over a lamp. It didn't break, but she felt as though *she* would, as though she'd simply fly apart with rage. Chunks of her would be scattered around the living room.

She tried to spank him, slapped his thigh. Her hand stung, pain radiating up her arm to her shoulder.

He was screaming, "You're killing me, Mommy!"

She was sure people closed up in their houses a block away could hear. *There's that woman abusing her little boy again.*

She let him go, and he ran to his room and slammed the door.

Christ, didn't she really, truly, more than anything in the world want to smash the little bastard's skull against the wall?

Instead she called her mother and cried about being a bad parent and asking whether she could drop Matt off after the parade and let him spend the night again.

While she was on the phone, Matt came out of his room and turned on "The Flintstones." Pamela remembered how Bobby would watch cartoons and say weird things like, "I'd love to pork that Betty Rubble bitch."

# Fifteen

When she pulls in her driveway, she can't help sitting a minute and staring at the carport, which leans to one side. There are several cracks around the stanchions. The carport is a constant reminder of Roy, who built it despite her protests. He was a plumber, not a carpenter, but that was a minor reason for her not wanting him to build it.

Seeing him at the parade today shook her up. He came right up to her, put Matt on his shoulders, and started talking as if they were just old pals, as if there were no mutilated hearts involved in their relationship. She asked how his fiancée was. After a couple of minutes he put Matt down and said it had been nice seeing them and walked away.

The house is quiet. It's nice this way. Matt likes staying with his grandma. She spoils him with junk food and toys and an unrestricted diet of violent TV, the way Roy did before Pamela pushed him out of her life.

The mess Matt made in the hall outside the bathroom is mostly still there. Pamela is aware that Roy saw her today without makeup. She used to worry about the way she looked to him. Sometimes she felt anger toward him. He didn't tell her to fix herself up. Just his existence in her life made her feel an obligation to look decent. Men were a pain in the ass, even when they didn't mean to be. She didn't even know how she felt about him; still she didn't want him thinking she was ugly. It was bad enough he didn't know her when she was thin.

She goes into the kitchen to do the pile of dishes Matt dirtied all day up till they left for the parade. After she finishes filling the sink with hot water, the quietness is eerie. The wind is whipping up outside. Rain and a cold front are moving in. Pamela worries about her own coldness. She wonders whether she really "got rid of" Roy or whether she lost him. Her feelings are too complicated to make sense.

The plates and silverware clink. She always pushes men away: Lon, Bobby, Roy. Her ears or the old house or both start playing their tricks. Out of the air comes one of Bobby's belches, as if from a distance. *Shit,* she hears. She shivers and plunges her hands into the hot water and closes her eyes to block out the sudden image of Bobby in a T-shirt holding his little pistol. *You don't love me no more, do you?* Is that why he did it? Or was it an accident? These are questions she has asked herself a million times.

Closing her eyes does no good, so she opens them and sees water trickling from around the cold-water faucet, which Roy was always trying to fix but never could.

Her name, *Pam*, bursts softly in the air, dissipates in a mist. *Pam*—another word that has made its way from where Bobby is.

# Sixteen

C rystal dreams about something Anita told her. She dreams of Anita stepping into a silver camper trailer shaped like a snail and catching her husband in bed with a fat girl. This happened, Anita said, when she was fourteen, a newlywed of two months. She grabbed her husband's BB gun and shot his eye out. She was aiming elsewhere else, she assured Crystal. Crystal doesn't know what Anita's husband looks like, but in her dream, he has bony shoulder blades and bright red pimples on his butt, and the girl has thighs like barrels. Then Anita is Crystal. It is Crystal who grabs a gun, but this one is not a BB gun; it looks more like a bazooka, and Anita's husband's head explodes all over the silver walls.

Crystal jerks awake, cold and sweaty.

After she remembers where she is, she gets off the cot

carefully and feels her way around in the dark for the candles and matches. There's a washbasin and jugs of water. She opens a jug and sniffs the water, then washes her face. She's glad there's no mirror to make her even more depressed than she already is. After she eats a can of fruit cocktail, she lies back down but can't sleep.

She picks up the darts on the floor and pulls the rest out of the dart board. She hasn't played darts since she was tiny, eight or nine, and she's surprised she's as good as she is. She tossed darts a lot earlier today, and now she's hooked the way people get hooked on playing video games or watching soap operas or anything else—hooked on drugs, on religion, on love. She backs up, aims at the red bull's-eye: Doc's heart.

Her and Doc's plan was sketched out in the stockroom at Kmart.

Doc said, "Listen, you want to go to lunch sometime?"

"Huh?"

"Eat. You know. And maybe . . . go for a drive or something?"

"Sure." She giggled for no reason. Her eyes moved quickly around the stockroom. She looked everywhere but at Doc. She worried that somebody might be listening behind one of the stacks of boxes.

"We'll take separate cars," he said.

"Sure."

"That way, if there was car trouble or something, nobody would . . ." He was shaking his head as if saying no to a question.

"Sure."

The next day she followed Doc's Chevrolet Caprice to Portsmouth. She drove her fifteen-year-old VW Bug, which her dad gave her on her sixteenth birthday. When she and

Scott Wilder were supposed to be preengaged, Scott had put a bumper sticker on the back saying, "Maybe! And that's final!" Doc didn't have any bumper stickers. Crystal had recently decided that people with class didn't put bumper stickers on their cars. Buck had a really dumb one on his rusty truck that said, "Farmers Can Plow Longer."

At a dark Italian restaurant Crystal took two bites of her lasagna, and that was all she wanted.

"What's wrong?" Doc asked.

"Nothing. This is nice. When I was in high school, dates usually took me to McDonald's all the time. One guy never took me anywhere else. He'd take me there and say, 'Anything you want. I mean it.' And he really thought he was giving me a big treat."

"Farmers." Doc snorted. Then he looked embarrassed. "Don't get me wrong. Nothing wrong with farmers."

"Yeah, well. Anyway I'm not a farmer. I grew up in town. My dad sells insurance."

Doc smiled. "All the boys you had coming around must have given your dad fits."

"He was always kind of shy with them, and I guess he spoiled me anyway. I could always get anything I wanted from my dad. If my mom didn't stop him. She's the one that kept me under control."

"You deserve to be spoiled. You're really beautiful."

"Thank you." She couldn't look at him. She sipped her Pepsi.

"A woman like you deserves to be happy. I hear you're not, though."

"Has Anita been talking to you?"

"She just wants to help."

Crystal looked down at her fingernails and thought about

scratching up Doc's back, marking her territory—a message to that fat nun. "I think everybody should do what they have to to be happy. Life's too short."

"You're absolutely right," Doc said. He waved his hand at her plate. "Eat."

She shook her head, smiling. Doc was cleaning his plate. She admired that. He wasn't nervous at all. He wasn't the kind of man who would start watching soap operas if his life fell apart. She took some ice into her mouth and started crunching it.

"So tell me," he said. "After we're through here, do you want to go somewhere?"

She shrugged. "I don't care."

"It's up to you."

"Whatever you want to do."

"Do you want to go back to Peebles?"

"No."

"Are you sure?"

"Yes." They gazed at each other. Crystal was the first to drop her eyes.

The waitress came and asked how things were. Doc said things were fine.

Crystal crunched on some more ice. She was shivering. "This girlfriend of mine got married her junior year? And she was all happy about it and everything, but then her husband got real weird on her. He wanted to send two hundred dollars to Oral Roberts because he thought it'd help him win a Datsun he had a raffle ticket for. They were real poor, and when she wouldn't let him have some money her mom gave her, he went out and got a switch off a tree and came back in their trailer and hit her across the face with it."

While she was trying to remember the point of telling

Doc this story, she bit down on an ice cube, and a shock of pain made her jerk.

"What's wrong?"

"Nothing," she said. She took a drink of her Pepsi and thought she'd scream. She'd broken a tooth, she would find out when she went to the dentist.

As she followed Doc to the motel, the pain subsided. There was just an annoying numbness, but when her tongue explored the left side of her mouth, she nearly ran off the road. "Great!" she said aloud. "Great!"

This kind of disaster wasn't new. A lot of her special occasions had been spoiled. When she was little, she got the flu or a bad cold almost every year on her birthday and Christmas Eve. The Halloween she was eight she had a fever of 104. She promised her mother she was going to sleep, but her mother stayed sitting on the edge of Crystal's bed, petting her head and saying, "Poor baby." Crystal finally screamed at her to leave her alone. As soon as her mother shut the door, Crystal got up and put on her Sleeping Beauty costume. She opened her window and unhooked the screen. Carrying a white pillowcase (she thought it would be inappropriate for Sleeping Beauty to carry an orange Halloween bag), she staggered across the lawn to the neighbors' house and rang the doorbell. When the door opened, the neighbor woman looked down at her with her eyes wide and said, "Child, are you all right?"

Crystal felt a bead of sweat drop off the end of her nose and whispered, "Trick or treat," then fainted.

Three days before her wedding she tripped over a lawn ornament, a small plaster deer, and got married wearing a cast on her arm. She had to remove the long sleeves from her dress, and she couldn't stop her friends from writing and drawing on the cast. There were names and hearts and flowers all

over her arm. Standing in front of the stern-faced old
preacher, she felt it was somehow worse than having obscene
tattoos or wearing a red dress. The friend whose husband had
hit her across the face with a switch took colored markers and
drew two little naked creatures with belly buttons and eyes so
huge they looked like mutants and labeled them "Luv Buddies." During the ceremony the preacher kept frowning at
Crystal's cast. He had a horrible, booming way of saying "God"
and "Eternity." Buck had sweat running down from his temples, and his face was bright pink like an old fat person with
high blood pressure, and he couldn't remember more than the
first three or four words of the lines he was supposed to say,
so Crystal had to mumble them out of the side of her mouth.
She was sure that any second the preacher was going to stop
the ceremony and say, "They don't have any business getting
married. She's just a child and he's a moron."

Following Doc's Caprice, she made several turns at crossroads. She didn't recognize anything. The motel he was taking
her to was way out in the country on a back road halfway
between Portsmouth and Athens. When she started getting
behind, Doc slowed down. Driving fast scared her.

There were a lot of creepy, run-down houses and trailers. The rusty shells of cars and trucks dotted the hilly land-
scape. Along one stretch of road, walking toward her, was a
gaunt, unshaven man with one arm, his empty sleeve fluttering
behind him. She had the impression he was staring at her as
she approached, and he had to step into the ditch suddenly because she didn't think to move to the left.

The motel was made up of six clapboard cabins. A faded
sign said, WE HAVE TV! Crystal stayed in her VW, but the door
to the office, which was one of the six cabins, was held open
with a rock, and she could watch a bent old man hand Doc a

key. It looked as though the old man was missing a couple of fingers.

Her tongue explored the bad tooth. When she jerked, her hand hit the horn, and the old man peered out at her, then said something to Doc, and they both laughed.

When she and Doc got inside their cabin, they discovered the door wouldn't lock from the inside. Doc just shrugged, but Crystal said she'd really like a door that locked. Doc took the one chair in the room, a wobbly wooden thing, and leaned it against the door. There were no curtains on the window, so Doc covered it with the threadbare blanket from the bed. The bathtub was full of tiny bugs that Doc said probably came from the tobacco patch behind their cabin. He said he'd take care of the problem. Then all he did was close the bathroom door.

With his three-piece suit off, Doc looked boyish. He had square, narrow shoulders, and his collar bones stuck out, but he had a bit of a spare tire around his waist you couldn't see when he had clothes on. His skin was milky white.

When they were both naked, they stood at the foot of the bed. He held her shoulders, and she lightly touched his waist. He still had his wristwatch on. After he kissed her, he told her he'd never known such a desirable woman. She liked the fact he called her a woman. Although she was twenty and had been married two years, everybody else still called her a girl. Lately Buck had been frequently asking, in a whiny voice, "You still my girl? You sure you ain't decided to be somebody else's girl?" She always told him to stop being stupid.

Now she felt a twinge of guilt, but Doc touched her face with one finger, and she said, "I love you, Doc. I'd die for you."

He looked startled. "No reason to do that."

"I'm sorry." The pain from her tooth was spreading into her cheek.

"Let's not talk." And he fell sideways onto the bed, taking her with him. The bed felt mushy. Ruined springs poked at her lower back. But Doc was good. He was gentle and slow, and the springs didn't matter. His hands were soft—the way, Crystal thought, a doctor's should be. He was a better lover than Buck, who tended to puff and sweat too much for her taste. Her tooth almost didn't matter; for a moment it actually didn't. Then her tongue went over there with a mind of its own. She gasped and wheezed, and Doc thought it was because of what he was doing. When he kissed her hard, she jerked her head away and shrieked. In a breathy voice he said, "You're incredible."

Doc got dressed fast, his back to her, and when he looked at her again, his eyes had changed; something had gone out of them. In his dark suit and with the distracted look on his face, he could have been getting ready to go to a funeral, Crystal thought.

She buttoned her blouse slowly. Her whole jaw throbbed. Doc went over and stood by the door, jingling his car keys. He was quiet until he said, "You like Stevie Nicks?"

"I guess. Sure."

"I'm going to her concert in Cincinnati tomorrow night."

"Yeah?"

"My wife and I and a couple of our friends. Jesus, I remember seeing her once about ten years ago when I was in college." Crystal thought for a moment he was talking about a time ten years ago when he saw his wife, but then he said, "She just danced up on the stage for twenty minutes at one point. Didn't sing a word. Just danced. And nobody was bored. Twirling around. Her hair. God." He was quiet again. He moved the chair away from the door. He said softly, as if to himself, "I love Stevie."

He drove fast. Crystal tried to keep up, but after her tires squealed on a couple of curves, she slowed down. It had gotten dark, and Doc's taillights dimmed, became mere pinpoints of red light, and eventually vanished.

At a crossroads she stopped and had no idea which way to go. Her jaw and head were both throbbing now. It had gotten cold, and her car's heater blew stale-smelling hot air onto her shins. She didn't understand why Doc was doing this to her. What had she done?

She looked to the right and to the left and straight ahead. She felt tears well up. She was suddenly very scared—and amazed to realize that she was living dangerously. She wasn't merely putting her marriage on the line (she suddenly wasn't sure at all that she wanted to leave Buck); it was more than that. Her recent behavior was making her vulnerable, turning her into the kind of woman who vanished and was never seen again, whose car was found by a lake or in a shopping-center parking lot in a city hundreds of miles from her home or at a crossroads way out in the middle of nowhere, the motor running maybe, the headlights on high beam, her purse on the passenger seat. Just vanished. A victim of carelessness, of a sloppy way of life. Ripe pickings for Evil. She had always been a good girl. She had been Miss Pumpkin Festival, for Christ's sake. Now . . .

A pickup truck, its lights glaring, came up behind her all of a sudden, and its horn blasted. She took a left and drove fast, her heart sprinting, her palms wet.

She was lost for hours. She envied the people inside the lit-up shacks and trailers she passed, but out of embarrassment and fear she didn't dare stop and ask for directions, for help.

She remembered rumors from her childhood about colonies of cutthroat hillbilly albinos. She kept glancing at her gas gauge. Finally she came to a familiar highway north of Athens. By the time she got home, her whole body hurt. She couldn't close her mouth completely. She let drool spill down her chin. She stumbled through her front door and found Buck asleep in his armchair. She shook him.

"Buck, you got to wake up."

"What?" He lifted his head, opened his eyes, and stared blankly at her. "You're back? What's wrong?"

She didn't know what to say.

"What happened?" he asked.

She backed away and knocked a cup off the end table. The handle on it broke off. She picked up the pieces. "I'll steal some glue."

"You'll get fired."

"What?"

"You'll get fired if you steal glue."

She suddenly knew what she wanted to say. "Buck, I wanta quit my job."

The next morning she called the manager at Kmart and told him she had to quit. She had to stay home, she said, to take care of her husband.

## Seventeen

Tired of his driving practice, Buck decides to head home. He drives slowly, not wanting to go to the trouble of trying to get into third gear. When he comes to his property, he pulls to the side of the gravel road. He gets out and looks at a field of ruined soybeans.

He gets an urge to take a walk out through the field and climbs the wobbly barbed-wire fence. He walks along, kicking plants, hearing nothing but the sucking sounds his boots make in the mud.

His dad said he should look into getting money from the government for letting his land lie fallow, but Buck has never liked the idea of getting paid for nothing. Next month, when the ground is dry enough to plow, he'll get to work, as always.

For the first week he was in the hospital, his dad helped

out, having come up from Atlanta. He sold Buck's five cows so that Buck wouldn't have to worry about them—Crystal certainly couldn't take care of them; she claimed cows scared her. Buck wanted the rest of the soybeans harvested, but his dad said he couldn't do it. He stood at the foot of Buck's hospital bed and said, "I would, but I'm sixty-eight years old, son, and I got arthritis so bad, I can't bend my fingers most mornings." He held up his hands and bent them to look like claws. Besides, he'd sold Buck's combine. He'd practically given it away, and Buck was furious, told his dad it was like shooting a perfectly good horse just because it threw you.

"I didn't think you'd ever want to see it again," his dad said.

"Shit! Shit, shit, shit!"

His dad paled and trembled.

Buck got on the phone and started calling around. An old farmer who lived down the road from Buck agreed to harvest Buck's horse corn for thirty percent of what it brought at market. His mouth was full of rotten teeth, and he needed money to get false ones, but he was too busy to do the soybeans and corn both.

Whenever Buck went to market, he got the impression that he was the only farmer in the county under the age of sixty. He'd try to join in a conversation with a group of farmers, but after he commented on the weather or market prices, he fell silent among those elderly men with their leathery skins, their missing fingers, and their reminiscences of droughts in 1952 and 1961 and of Walt somebody and Ervin and Henry, who'd been dead twenty, thirty, forty years, crushed under tractors that tipped over on wicked hills.

Buck's mother didn't come up from Atlanta with his dad. She was busy helping with his brother Buddy's new baby. It was Buddy and his wife's fifth. Buck didn't care—hell, no, not really, not *really*—that his mother didn't come. She probably would have sat by his bed, reading a book about some ancient or dead movie star, insisting on staying by his side but ignoring him with her nose stuck in her book or, worse, complaining constantly about how hospital smells gave her headaches and speculating about what hideous diseases lurked behind doors marked "Isolation"—or, worst, telling Buck that with all his blood transfusions he'd better start worrying about AIDS.

And she would have talked about Buddy—how Buddy's house had a spiral staircase and how he'd just bought a new Lincoln Continental and how his twelve-year-old was going to skip seventh grade and how the new baby looked like the one on Gerber baby-food jars.

When Crystal gave birth to a stillborn, Buck's mother said on the phone from Atlanta that it was just never meant to be. "Maybe God knew it would have had a bad life." She paused; then, flustered, she rushed on: "Not to say anything against you and Crystal. That's not what I meant. That's not what I meant at all. God knows you would have tried."

Buck had painted his old room and bought a secondhand crib and refinished it. He had built shelves to put toys on. After the baby was born dead, Crystal kept the door of that room closed all the time. She said she didn't think she'd ever want to put a baby in there. She knew there wasn't any logical reason, but the room gave her the creeps. She tried to explain to Buck that the room seemed haunted because, throughout her pregnancy, she had vividly imagined her baby in there watching a mobile, playing with blocks, dressing dolls.

Buck pauses in his walk and looks around at the brown fields, then at his stump and rubs it. It's sore from pushing and knocking the gear-shift lever. He doesn't keep it bandaged anymore. The doctor said Buck didn't have to, and the bandages were hot and scratchy. The stump doesn't look as bad as it used to, but it's never going to be a pretty sight. An artificial hand covered by a glove is his best bet, he figures.

It suddenly occurs to him that if he gets good at driving, he still might not want to go anywhere. He would prefer to hide on his farm. He dreads just the thought of having to go to a store. When he has had to go to the doctor's, people have stared, then caught themselves and looked away fast. Little kids say to their parents, "Where's that man's hand?" Or they just say, "Look!" and jab their fingers in his direction.

Since Crystal moved out, she has brought him groceries once a week. She never says much. "I got you Swanson potpies even though you said to get those cheap kind. The Swansons are worth the money. If you need anything, you call that number I left."

He always stands across the room, watching her put food away. He barely speaks, feels mute around her. He just nods or shakes his head.

"And, Buck, I got to say it again. Please stop sending me flowers. I feel bad enough without you sending me flowers. You understand?"

He nods. Then as soon as she's gone, he picks up the phone and calls the florist.

If she never lives with him again, if they divorce and she marries the real estate agent or someone else, maybe she'll still bring him groceries, and he'll be able to keep hiding.

But he's lonely too. He thinks again about the artificial hand with a glove over it, tries to picture it. It wouldn't be so bad to be able to drive over to Brown County to the Kountry Klub and pick up a woman. He'd take her to a motel in case Crystal decided to come home—in love with him again; he wouldn't want to mess that up. Maybe some woman at the Kountry Klub—there to get picked up anyway—wouldn't be bothered by his stump. Hell, he might not even care if she made love to him out of pity. Maybe some women would think it was kinky.

He swallows, remembering the feel and taste of sucking a nipple.

One night not long after he got home from the hospital, he tried to improvise a hand by pulling a glove stuffed with toilet paper on over his stump. Crystal was trying to be sweet, trying to keep her eyes on his face, and he got her to take off her heavy, old-lady's robe, and her neck flushed the way it always did when she got worked up. She had her hand on the back of his neck, and he had her hard nipple in his mouth. Then his hand fell off, landing on the floor beside the bed with the soft slap of a small pillow, and she screamed. Her face and neck went white.

That was a bad night, but not as bad as the night he thought she would never come home. At two in the afternoon she left for her job at Kmart in Peebles. She usually got home around ten, but at midnight she still hadn't shown up, and he got no answer when he called Kmart. She was still gone at two in the morning when he drifted off to sleep in his armchair, tears drying on his cheeks and chin, certain he'd never see her again: She had run off with another man, or she was dead in her yellow Volkswagen. He imagined a disaster of twisted steel and shattered glass, the black night quiet except for the drip of transmission fluid and the hiss of a busted radiator, the sky full of long, pointed stars.

He touches the bruise he got on his chin when it hit the steering wheel. Then he looks up at the sky, doesn't see Jesus. The day the combine took his hand, Jesus was up there, looking the way he did years ago in the picture high on the wall of Buck's Sunday school class.

Thinking of Jesus and of his loneliness and horniness, Buck cannot help thinking of Amy Hanky. When he was a senior in high school, she was a freshman, and one day in the spring she sat down next to him in the cafeteria and told him to come over to her house; she wanted to show him something. Buck knew what she wanted to show him. She'd made the same invitation to eight or ten other boys since the beginning of the school year. She was the inspiration for most of the artwork on the walls of the boys' john.

She lived in a wreck of a house with her old man, who was a famous drunk. For years, late on Friday nights, he had directed traffic in front of the courthouse in West Union and staggered along the streets calling his dead wife's name or yelling that the mayor was a fag, that he'd seen the man in a bar in Portsmouth holding hands with black boys.

In Amy's front yard there was a big tractor tire painted pink with a variety of flowers growing in the center of it. At the end of the driveway, at the foot of the mailbox, was an old toilet sitting crooked, the words JUNK MAIL painted in runny black letters on the tank and an arrow pointing to the bowl.

Amy was pencil-thin and pale. Her thighs were hardly bigger than Buck's arms. Her hair was a dull black. On her bed she wrapped her arms and legs around Buck, surprised him with her strength, and came three times before he did. Then she wouldn't let go.

"Say you love me," she said. Her face was sweaty. Buck noticed black flecks in her green eyes. "Say you love me, and I'll let you go." Buck didn't say anything. He tried to get loose, but they just rolled around locked together. "Just say it." He mumbled it, and she let him get up.

While he dressed, she lay on her bed staring at the ceiling. Cracks crisscrossed it. The walls of her room were covered with crumbling and peeling green wallpaper that had goldfish on it. The window shades were so old, they had turned yellow. There was a crucifix on one wall and a poster of Elvis Presley and another of Bruce Springsteen.

When Buck was almost fully dressed, she said, "If you look at my ceiling real close, you can see the face of Jesus."

He laughed. He was thinking about all the other girls he wanted to screw, and he was already thinking about coming back to Amy for more practice. "That why you were yellin', 'Oh, God. Oh, God. Oh, God'?"

She looked at him, her eyes wide. "Yes. It was. I was letting him know I knew."

Buck zipped up his fly. "Knew what?"

"Knew he was watching."

Buck looked at the cracked ceiling. "Hell—"

"Jesus was watching us. You can't hide from God. He saw what you did. But it's all right 'cause you said you love me." Then she went back to staring at the ceiling.

Buck ran his fingers through his hair. He looked at her body. She was fifteen, but she looked about twelve. He decided he was never touching her again.

"Jesus Christ's face on my ceiling," she said. "It got clearer and clearer all while I was growing up. I used to ask him for Barbie dolls and nice dresses and patent-leather shoes. Now I ask him for boys. He gets *them* for me. Before Mama died, I showed her the ceiling. And she laid right here, coughing up blood and little pieces of her insides, and watched Jesus watching her."

In the moments after the combine ripped his hand off, Buck stood in the middle of the soybean field, and the tractor's engine and the noise of the combine became a terrible roar that made the air heavy and hard to breathe. He put his left hand over his mutilated wrist, feeling dizzy and nauseated. He just stood there. Soon he was ready to give up, to fall down and rest—to let all his blood soak into the earth. Then he looked up, and there was Jesus' face hovering way up near the sun, and Buck ran for the road. Terrified.

# Eighteen

On the straight stretch to his driveway Buck shrugs and
says out loud, "What the hell," and bumps the gear-shift
lever into second, keeps accelerating, bumps into third, then
goes for fourth.

He zips past his driveway doing sixty, a wake of dust behind him like a jet trail. Victory.

He slows to turn around in a neighbor's driveway. He
holds up his stump and hollers a joyous "Yes!" the way he does
when he watches football games on TV and the Cincinnati
Bengals score. He feels himself make a fist, although he has no
hand. He has to look at his stump twice. A phantom fist. He
has to remind himself that he's in a dream he'll never wake up
from.

# Nineteen

Even with cable TV Pamela has discovered there's nothing to watch on Saturday night. It seems the networks don't care about Saturday nights; everybody's out on the town, they assume, except all the losers—fat, pimply kids who can't get dates and old people who go to bed early.

She could go to the new video rental store in Peebles, but a storm has blown in suddenly and it's pouring rain. Besides, video stores depress her. She always sees row after row of movies that remind her of one of the men she's been involved with. In a way she'd like to see *Back to the Future* again, but she'd be thinking of Bobby the whole time. All the recent movies remind her of Roy. The older ones conjure up memories of Lon. So do all the baseball movies: *Bull Durham, Major League, Eight Men Out.*

It's about this time, around eight o'clock, when Roy would usually come over.

"Kid stuffed her teddy bear down these people's toilet." Pamela smiles, remembering. "Thing got lodged in the line. I been diggin' in the dark so these people could run water when they get up in the mornin'. I'm sorry I'm late."

Pamela admired the way Roy really seemed to care about people whose plumbing acted up. "They paid me tonight too. Look at that." He held the check with both hands. His thumbs were big, the nails yellow and cracked, although he'd been a plumber only a few months. "Two hundred and fifty dollars. I'm gonna give you that Christmas present I was talkin' about."

"Now, hold on, Roy."

"I'm gonna build you a carport before Christmas."

"Roy, that's too big a thing. Just get a bottle of perfume or some pot holders. Something little."

"I'm gonna build you a two-car carport, girl."

"I only got one car."

He winked, grinned.

She thought of his shiny black Grand Prix with chrome mags. She wondered what people thought when he drove up after they had called a plumber. He kept his tools in the trunk.

"You ought to use that money to buy some more of the tools you need if you're going to get serious about the plumbing business."

"I'm serious."

Roy had been a sales representative for years for a company that manufactured bush hogs, but the company had gone out of business. He had just started working as a plumber when Pamela met him. "My daddy was a plumber," he told her. "He taught me all I need to know. 'Bein' a plumber is as

good as bein' an undertaker,' Daddy used to say. 'Everybody
dies, and everybody's pipes bust.' "

Whenever they sat at the kitchen table, the dim light and
the shadows made Roy look old. He was forty and had a
twenty-one-year-old son from a teenage marriage. Roy's bushy
beard was streaked with gray.

"How's the hot-water faucet?" he might ask.

"The cold-water faucet is leaking now."

"I just fixed the hot-water one."

"Yeah, but you didn't fix the cold-water one."

"I should have. I'm sorry."

"Oh, Roy, you're not obligated to do anything for me."

They stared at each other.

"Come on, Pam," he said, reaching over, trying to tickle
her. "What's keepin' us from gettin' married?"

Pamela slapped his hand away, embarrassed that he could
feel the rolls that formed around her waist when she sat down.
She stood up and opened the refrigerator and looked in at a
diet Coke.

"Tell me now."

"Oh, shut up, Roy."

"Why you so snappy? How was Matt today?"

"Awful. I don't know what I'm going to do with him. I'm
afraid he's going to end up in jail."

"He's only a kid," Roy said, grinning. He got up, a big
bear of a man, and came toward her.

"I mean when he grows up."

Roy reached out and slapped a cabinet door. The kitchen
cabinets were painted yellow. There was an STP sticker on
one, a Rock 97 sticker on another, put there, Pamela supposed, by the people she bought the house from. "I'm gonna

strip and paint these cabinets," Roy said. "After I build your carport."

"I'll do that myself, when I get a chance. Matt would just ruin them probably. Draw on them or something."

"I love you," Roy said.

"I . . . I was talking about . . . the child."

"The child? You make him sound like a Stephen King book."

"You know what he's been saying lately when people ask him what he wants to be when he grows up? He says he doesn't want to be anything. I think he needs professional help. Look." She shows him teeth marks on her forearm.

"That don't mean he's going to be the next Charlie Manson."

"He's got the look, just like that guy in that TV movie."

"Ah, now. Matt's a fine-lookin' boy."

Pamela felt a rush of guilt. Tears welled up. She leaned back heavily against the counter, which pressed into her fleshy lower back. God, she'd gotten fat. Roy gathered her into his arms. She felt smothered in his beard and big arms and soft chest. It was as if he were pushing a pillow into her face.

"Let me be a daddy to him. That's all he needs. I never hardly saw my boy after he was Matt's age 'cause my ex-wife moved to Arizona with that computer programmer. Matt told me he liked me."

She pushed him away. " 'Cause you spoil him with toys and junk food."

"I like to spoil people," he said softly. And he gave her a sad look.

Pamela liked Roy's eyes. They were blue and full of love—she couldn't deny that. He looked like a boy, a little like

Lon when she loved him, when she was seventeen and thought she would have gladly died for him. She fought that girl still inside her.

Sometimes she thought she loved Roy or could learn to if she let herself, if she could forget the way Lon disappointed her and the way Bobby turned weird and mean on her.

She met Roy when he was in the hospital for a prostate operation. Pamela had been a licensed practical nurse for three years. It was better than her old job at McDonald's over-all. It took her just a year at the junior college in Portsmouth to become an LPN. It paid better than McDonald's, but she'd discovered that there were worse things than half-eaten Big Macs and people angry about their fish fillets. At McDonald's there was a lot less blood and puke and shit and death than at the county hospital. A young farmer had come in in October with his whole hand torn off.

Roy was humiliated by his prostate problem. He kept his bed sheet pulled up to his chin, as if to cover the thick chest hairs sprouting from the top of his hospital gown. He stared at the ceiling when Pamela had to lift the sheet to check on things.

The first thing she ever said to him was, "You're awful young for this kind of operation."

He hardly said a word until the day he left the hospital. Fully dressed, his boots on, towering over her, he invited her to the Kountry Klub for a night out. She said she didn't think she could, but then he gave her one of his boyish looks. His eyes got to her, she had to admit. And she hadn't dated since Bobby killed himself. Four years without sex, the other nurses were always telling her, was something they could not comprehend.

Pamela didn't like the Kountry Klub at first. It was a

smokey, loud place with tacky wagon-wheel chandeliers. All
the smoke and rowdy people made her think of writhing souls
in hell. But a boy named Lloyd could sing ballads so sweet the
stiff-whiskered truckers and trashy women shut up and gazed
at the small stage area where Lloyd sat on a stool. They let
their cigarettes dangle from their lower lips, their eyes glazed
over. With his music Lloyd told stories of lost love and regrets,
and everybody in the place knew what he was talking about.

He made the people in the Kountry Klub fall in love or
think they were, and Pamela went home with Roy and let him
make love to her. She was angry with herself for weeks afterward: She'd become one of those women who have sex because of a song or a movie. Pamela knew a girl in high school
who let herself get laid every time a guy took her to a Clint
Eastwood film. The girl giggled in the lunchroom about how
Clint just put her in the mood and she was helpless to do anything about it. Pamela thought the girl was an idiot.

Whenever she and Roy made love, even if Matt was at
her mother's, she made him leave afterward. She never let him
sleep at her house. But often, after he was gone, she let her
robe fall on the floor, and she studied her body in the mirror
on the door of her bedroom closet. Her thighs were stout; her
breasts drooped. When she was eighteen and the bride of a
boy who seemed destined for stardom as a professional baseball player, Pamela thought about getting modeling jobs. In
high school she would sunbathe in her parents' front yard, and
boys in their hot rods would circle the block all afternoon.

Now she was a tub. But Roy always caressed her gently
and murmured to her that she was beautiful, that she was perfect. *You're a nut,* she wanted to say, but she never had the
breath to say it.

# Twenty

A week after Crystal quit her job at Kmart, Anita showed up at her house. "What are you doing here?" Crystal asked, meeting Anita in the yard only a few feet from Anita's car. She didn't want Buck to talk with her; Anita could ruin Crystal's life with one slip of her tongue. Crystal looked back at the house, and there was Buck standing in the front door with a quizzical expression on his face. "It's just somebody I know from Kmart," she said, and he nodded and backed into the house but left the door open.

"So that's old Buck, huh?" Anita said.

"How did you know where I lived?" Crystal was hugging herself because it was cold and she didn't have a coat on.

"Asked around. I wanted to see how you were doing. I know things didn't work out between you and Doc."

"I decided I didn't want to ruin my life," Crystal said in a low voice.

"So you and Buck are lovebirds again?"

"Well, I wouldn't say that."

"I said to Doc the other day, 'Well, Doc, what you think of Crystal quitting her job all of a sudden?' And he says, 'Who?' And I said, 'Crystal. You know.'"

Crystal looked back at the house, wishing Anita would keep her voice down.

"Doc said, 'So she quit. So what?' You know what I think? I think—"

Buck came to the door and said, "You want me to put the potpies in for supper?"

"Yeah, go ahead, honey," Crystal said.

"I haven't had a potpie in twenty years, I bet," Anita said. "Me and Earl live in a camper that just has a hot plate. We eat a lot of soup and McDonald's, but you know, McDonald's is getting expensive."

Crystal thought Anita might be trying to get an invitation to stay for dinner. "I hate to cook," Crystal said. She walked toward Anita's old GTO, which had made a lot of noise coming up the long driveway. It didn't have a front bumper. The hood and one fender were gray, but the rest of the car was orange.

Anita followed her, saying, "I found out Doc didn't really go to medical school. Tim in Automotive says Doc flunked out of veterinary school."

"I got to go," Crystal said.

"You're not happy. I can tell. I'm coming by Saturday night and taking you out."

"You call first. Okay?"

# Twenty-one

Getting involved with Doc was partly Anita's fault, and so was getting hooked up with Lon. Anita called the Saturday after she'd been to Crystal's house. About an hour before the phone rang, Crystal walked into the bathroom and caught Buck changing the bandages he kept wrapped around his stump—and for a split second, before turning away, she saw something that looked bloated and was several different sickening colors, a horrible rainbow—so she told Anita yes, she wanted to go out.

Anita liked to gun her GTO's engine, and in general she drove like a man, Crystal thought. She braked for stop signs at the last second and passed anybody who wasn't going over the speed limit. On the steering wheel her hands were big and veiny like a man's. Crystal had seen the thick veins in her skinny arms once when Anita wore a short-sleeve smock to work.

They cruised the main strip of Peebles, past the Pizza Hut, the McDonald's, the Big Boy restaurant, and the Taco Bell. A lot of high school kids were out, and for a moment, catching sight of a car full of cute boys, Crystal felt some of the excitement she used to feel when she and her girlfriends in high school fixed themselves up and cruised the strip, showing themselves off and teasing carloads of horny guys.

Anita drove down a side street and showed Crystal where she lived—an old silver camper sitting in the corner of a parking lot full of mud puddles. Crystal didn't know what Anita expected her to say. It was tacky and pathetic. Next to the lot was a run-down frame house with a hand-painted sign out front saying, CHURCH OF THE RISEN SAVIOR, ELVIS HAYWOOD, PASTOR. Crystal figured Elvis Haywood was the kind of preacher who made God sound like a bully who would beat the shit out of you if you didn't toady up to Him every second of the day.

"That's my daddy's church," Anita said. "Lord, if he knew some of the things I've done. Daddy takes his religion real serious. Breaks his heart he's lousy at faith healing. He's real jealous of faith healers on TV 'cause they're always so good. When I was little, he used to bring home sickly animals to practice on. He found something in the Bible that convinced him animals had souls, and he used to get into fights about it all the time with people. He'd put his hand on a dog or cat's forehead and say, 'God, rid this poor beast of its afflictions.' A raccoon bit off the end of his finger one time. But I swear to you he got rid of a stray dog's fleas and a cat's eye infection. But he never had any luck healing human beings. I remember one time Daddy felt sure he had the power—he'd just gotten rid of that dog's fleas—and he made an old lady hobble up to the front of the church with her walker, and he laid hands on her and shouted, and her eyelids fluttered like crazy. There for a second it was real scary, and I was thrilled for Daddy, but then he snatched her walker away, and she fell flat on her face. Broke her wrist trying to break the fall. Her son threatened to sue, but he got killed in a car wreck. When Daddy heard about the wreck, he hollered, 'Praise Jesus!' "

As they drove out of town into the countryside, Anita talked about how Doc was putting the moves on a new girl at the Kmart. Crystal wished she'd shut up about it. Finally Anita did. Crystal noticed they were passing the Star-Lite Drive-in Theater, which went out of business last year. The lot looked weird with the speakers gone from the poles and the screen just a big blank in the sky. Scott Wilder used to take her there to see horror movies. He'd keep his eyes on the teenage actors getting mutilated while he worked his hand into her pants.

After being quiet for a minute Anita eyed Crystal as if sizing her up. "I don't tell many people this, but I'm a witch."

"A what?"

"I'm a white witch. We're not into Satan worshiping or anything like that, although some of the girls in the coven have recently gotten kind of interested in it in a mild way."

Crystal said, "Oh?" She looked at Anita. The light from the dashboard cast a dim-green glow up onto her big nose.

"You know the wife of the president of the Peebles First National Bank?"

"No."

"Good. Then I can tell you. Well, she just joined our coven. We only let her 'cause we needed a thirteenth. She wears all these gaudy diamonds and giggles all the time. She's got these fat little hands with big rings all over them that remind me of a baby's hands. She wanted to know when we were going to teach her how to turn her husband into a toad. I guess rich women can afford to be stupid. Anyway she's in the coven, and a couple of housewives and a third-grade teacher and a woman dentist—"

"There aren't any women dentists around here." It occurred to Crystal that maybe Anita was joking. Maybe she should laugh.

"She's from Portsmouth."

"Right. Sure."

"We're planning to conjure up a famous person at our next sabbat. We've been trying for a while, but we think we've figured out the right formula now."

"That's real funny, Anita. Where we going?"

"I thought we'd head over to the Kountry Klub. But really, Crystal, we're going to give conjuring another try. This one girl, Amy Hanky—"

"Amy Hanky! I went to high school with Amy Hanky. She graduated when I was a sophomore."

"Uh-oh. I'm not supposed to reveal the names of any of the witches. You won't tell anybody, will you?"

"No."

"Thanks."

"Amy Hanky had a reputation for being a big sleaze."

"She is. She's always wanting to conjure up people like Elvis Presley and Jim Morrison. But I don't know what good she thinks that would do. I think she just wants to see if she can get laid by a spirit. We're supposed to be white witches. We're supposed to help people and make the world a better place. This girl Becky and me and a girl Cindy are thinking of breaking away from the others."

Crystal still didn't know what to think. "Who you want to bring back from the dead?"

"I like the idea of a president. We tossed around Abraham Lincoln, but Amy said it sure would be nice to go for a president with a little more sex appeal, and that banker's wife said what about Warren G. Harding, that he was even from Ohio, but we decided on President Kennedy. And I've got to admit that would be a thrill. You weren't born yet, but I remember him. I remember I'd drawn a picture on the kitchen wall of my cat which got run over, and it was in black crayon that wasn't about to wash off the wallpaper, and my mama took one of my daddy's belts to me. She was whipping me on my legs and back with that belt. Then all of a sudden it came on the radio that the president had been killed, and my mama just broke down and bawled and held me and rocked me. She kept kissing the top of my head."

They were in Mount Orab now. Up ahead were the neon lights of the Kountry Klub.

"What are you supposed to do with a spirit after you conjure him up?"

"Ask him for advice about personal problems and . . ."

Crystal's head was swimming. She felt as if she were going to go crazy listening to this talk. "You're going to ask John F. Kennedy for advice about personal problems?"

"Well, yeah, I guess."

"Like what?"

"I don't know."

"What you say? 'Mr. Dead President, I got this problem. Every month I have this real heavy flow . . .'?"

"He's not a gynecologist, for Christ's sake. You can ask him about how to solve world problems too. Let's just go in the club. I'm sorry I talked about all that stuff. Sometimes I just want to tell somebody about it."

The Kountry Klub was crowded. Smoke hung thick

around the wagon-wheel chandeliers. Most of the women looked trashy, Crystal thought. The men looked rough, like truck drivers and mill workers. A guy with a guitar sat on a stool on a little stage and sang country songs.

Crystal and Anita sat at a table with a red-and-white checkerboard tablecloth. "You come here a lot?" Crystal asked.

"Every once in a while. I met a guy here a couple of years ago that I had an affair with. Earl had his flings. One night I got mad at him about something—he wanted to watch wrestling when there was a real good movie on like *Terms of Endearment*, I think—and I got to thinking about how he'd always treated me bad, cheated on me a couple of times and was always making messes like when he'd eat Cheese Puffs and wipe his orange fingers on the sofa. He was sitting there watching wrestling and fartin' real loud and not letting me watch my show, so I told him I was going to go over to my daddy's house and watch my movie, but I knew Daddy'd be watching wrestling too. What I really did, of course, was went out and got laid. Sure made me feel better about life." Anita took a drink of her beer, then looked around. "Well, you see anybody interesting? Men, I mean."

"I don't—" Crystal glanced around. "That guy over there looks familiar for some reason."

"Who?"

Crystal pointed at a tall, lean, good-looking man slumped down in his chair, his legs stretched out, several empty beer mugs in front of him. He didn't look like anybody else in the place because he had on a suit, a green one.

"You know him?" Anita asked.

"I don't know."

"Well, let's find out." Anita stood up.

"Wait! I'm sure I don't know him. He looks drunk."

Anita didn't say anything. She went over and leaned down to talk into the guy's ear. He looked confused. Then Anita pointed at Crystal, who felt her face flush with hot blood. Crystal shook her head and waved Anita back to their table. The guy sat up. He really was good-looking. Then he smiled at her.

Suddenly Crystal felt frantic. There was a buzz in her ears as if an alarm clock had gone off in her head. She was horrified and euphoric. She knew she was about to fall in love. Again.

# Twenty-two

L loyd's new washing machine just makes a loud buzzing noise, will do nothing else. He doesn't know when he'll be able to sit home an entire day waiting for the Sears man. He stares at a pile of dirty clothes and tries to remember where he saw a Laundromat in his new neighborhood.

He sighs, tired from working all day. Some of the crowd that came to West Union for the parade spilled over into other towns in the county. His McDonald's in Portsmouth was a zoo all afternoon. Yuppie types from Cincinnati were dragging their kids around out here in the sticks to find antique stores and to show them what tobacco plants looked like. McDonald's, though, was the most interesting part of the day for the kids, he could tell.

He stuffs two pillowcases with jeans and underwear and

the dress shirts he wears at McDonald's. Since becoming the assistant manager of the McDonald's in Portsmouth, he makes a decent living and recently bought a small house that has a new furnace and that is over half a mile from the river. But he sometimes wonders what Jenny would think of him giving up his dream of making it as a country singer.

Most nights he lies in bed in his underwear, his guitar across his lap, and sings ballads about loneliness. He used to play at clubs and bars—like the Mad Dog, the Kountry Klub, and Sly's Saloon—almost every night for ten or fifteen dollars or for free just to get the experience. Jenny had to clean people's houses so they could eat. She broke out in hives every time she had to call her father and beg for money. Lloyd would sit by the phone with her, coaching her. "Tell him you got robbed," he'd whisper, but Jenny would shoo him away. He'd go out in his yard and toss rocks into the river. When he went back inside, he'd find her on their broken-down sofa wrapped in a blanket, looking at the fuzzy picture on the black-and-white TV, her face splotchy. They had both just graduated from high school, and Jenny's belly was a cannonball weighing her down.

Despite everything, she told him she never wanted him to give up his music. When they watched "Hee Haw," she'd say, "You'll be on there one of these days." And she said, "When you make a video of your song 'Lovely but Alone,' I want to be in it. I'll wear a frilly blue dress and sit on a white porch swing. And don't laugh but I think I could do it real well—I'll express the emotions of your song with my eyes. You always say I have soulful eyes."

If she were alive, Jenny would say he had sold out for a career in grease-burger world, but Lloyd imagines flashing his checkbook at her and saying, "Remember that Monte Carlo you wanted?" She'd like that. She'd also understand that he wants Cole, their little boy, back. Cole is with Jenny's parents in Florida, where they moved after Jenny's old man sold his hardware store. Lloyd could kick himself for letting Jenny's parents take Cole, but at the time, two years ago, Lloyd didn't think he could take care of even himself—not with Jenny gone.

# Twenty-three

Laundry Land is brightly lit and clean. Lloyd's got the whole place—rows of washers and dryers, plastic chairs all along the walls—to himself. Outside, the Saturday-night traffic plows through the flooded streets, kids three or four years younger than Lloyd with nothing to worry about but whether they're getting laid enough—because it really is hard to believe when you're seventeen that anything else is as important. Every once in a while thunder cracks. Rain has been coming down in sheets for two hours, and Lloyd's glad he doesn't have to worry about the river anymore. One stormy night when he and Jenny and Cole lived in a low-rent house on the bank of the river, it came inside while they were sleeping. Lloyd got up and stood at the top of the stairs, amazed by the sight of Cole's stuffed animals and building blocks floating around the living room, bumping softly into furniture. He had never lived on the river before, didn't know how fast it could be. They lived fifteen miles from Portsmouth; there were no neighbors to warn them. After deciding not to go downstairs for fear of getting electrocuted, he looked out the upstairs windows. His house was an island.

The river climbed the stairs, and in the late afternoon he and Jenny and Cole climbed out a window onto the porch roof. People driving on the road on the hill above them pointed at them, honked their horns, waved; Lloyd could see big grins on some of the people's faces. He remembered hearing of houses being lifted off their foundations in bad floods, like the one back in '37; he thought he remembered a picture in a history book showing a man riding his house down the river. Lloyd hugged his family. Jenny's hair was plastered to her head; her ears stuck out. Cole hid under her yellow raincoat, the front of it bulging the way it did when she was pregnant with him (her senior year of high school she had trouble squeezing into the desks). Lloyd held his family and looked out over the dark river and believed the only thing he could let himself believe at the time: that if you loved someone or something enough, it could never slip away.

# Twenty-four

A red-headed woman kicks the door of the Laundromat open and lugs in a plastic laundry basket overflowing with jeans and white uniforms. Her face is flushed, and her eyes are startling blue. She looks a little like Donna, who works at Lloyd's McDonald's. Donna has three kids (although she's only twenty-one), but she looks good. She reminds Lloyd of the big-bosomed women on the covers of novels at the Kroger supermarket, except her teeth are crooked; they're slanted in all directions like old tombstones. In the last month Lloyd's taken her to dinner three times and gone with her to her church twice. Lloyd barely knew her in high school. She had a reputation for being wild. Smoked, drank, wore tight clothes. An easy lay. She had thick, fuzzy, long red hair that trailed behind her like a banner. Then right after she got divorced, she joined a fundamentalist church. Now she has stiff little curls that feel sticky when Lloyd touches them. She has a bumper sticker on the back of the Camaro she got out of the divorce that says, "I Talked to God Today," and another that says, "Happiness Is Knowing I'm Going to Heaven." It reminds Lloyd of a bumper sticker a friend of his used to have on his pickup truck; there was a cartoon cat squeezed into a bottle, and the caption read, "Happiness Is a Tight Pussy." Lloyd thinks a lot about the things he'd like to do to Donna, but she won't have sex, she says, until she's married again.

Until four months ago Donna kept insisting that if Lloyd joined her church, Jenny would come back. God would bring her back. God could do anything. A dozen times or more she repeated the story about an old farmer at her church who had his nose eaten off by cancer, and after the congregation prayed for him, he grew a new one.

The day Jenny disappeared, she left in the morning to clean an old lady's house while Lloyd stayed home with Cole. He doesn't remember what she said before she left, if anything. He was trying to finish a new song, and she knew to leave him alone. He's sure she would have kissed Cole, who was still sleeping. Later in the morning he tried to get Cole to say "Daddy" but he'd only say "Momma." They watched TV, and they waited for Jenny to come home.

A month later Jenny's car was found in Kentucky. Her purse was in the trunk. Then four months ago, after two years, a farmer in Tennessee hunting in his woods for a stray cow about to give birth found a human skeleton.

# Twenty-five

"Hey, are you really down there?" It's Anita. "I called last night, and Lon told me you were in the bomb shelter." Crystal considers staying quiet, hoping she'll go away. "Did he beat you up?"

"You're as bad as my mother," Crystal says.

"Take it from me. All men are pig shit."

"Lon didn't beat me up. I came down here to think."

"I just got off work and had to come out and tell you something."

"You can tell me, but I don't want to come out. Just tell me through this thing."

"Well, okay. The thing is I caught Earl with a woman yesterday."

"I'm sorry."

"I guess he thought I was working later or something 'cause I walk in and there he is with some old bag."

"A what?"

"An old lady. She looked old enough to be his grand-mother. She had gray hair, and her tits were all shriveled up. She starts screamin' at *me*, like *I'm* the one that's done some-thing wrong. She came swinging her fists at me like a lunatic escapee from an old-folks home or something, and she tripped over one of Earl's boots, and her goddamn false teeth popped out. I swear I never saw such a sight. Her teeth were laying there on their side on my red shag rug all slimy looking, and she starts crying real pathetic like, and I'm thinking this is all Earl's fault. The son of a bitch. That bastard came toward me with his arms out. 'Oh, baby, you don't understand.' With his silly crooked dick wagging. I swear he's got the longest, crookedest dick on any man alive. Looks like . . . like a mon-key's tail. The first time I saw it, I thought . . . it might be . . . be what Daddy meant when he hollered in church about the mark of the beast."

Crystal realizes suddenly that Anita is crying. "I'm real sorry, Anita."

"I was truly scared of it. I was. I was only fourteen, and I'd only seen a couple of pictures and some boy's in third grade. But I *knew* Earl's thing was not normal. It was too long and crooked. I ruined our honeymoon 'cause I was so scared. I kept talking about how wonderful it was that our souls were joined together for eternity. 'We'll walk in heaven hand in hand a million years from now,' I said to him, and I kept talk-ing, and he was kissing me and feeling me all over, and I said, 'Wait! You got to promise me something,' and out the corner of my eye I was looking at that long crooked thing I thought would probably kill me for sure, and I said to him, 'If I die early in life like my mama, I want you to cremate me and mix some of my ashes in a glass of water and drink it.' I told him that was what my daddy did. And he said, 'Will you shut up?' And I said, 'This is serious. We all die. You'll die someday. So will all your brothers and sisters and your daddy and your mama.' And he told me to shut up again, but I couldn't 'cause I was so nervous and scared, and his dick started shrinking, and I thought if it shrunk enough, then maybe it wouldn't hurt. I said, 'You never know when you'll die. You can be alive one minute and dead as a doornail the next. We could die tomorrow or today. Daddy says we're all just like caterpillars. If we're lucky, we become butterflies, but sin is like a giant's foot that smashes us into nothing but green guts.' Then Earl groaned, and his dick looked like the eraser on a pencil."

Crystal doesn't know what to say. She hears Anita blowing her nose violently. She stares at the candles on the card table. Finally she says, "I'm nobody to talk, but he deserves . . ." But she doesn't know what he deserves.

"I got something to show you. I made him pay, don't worry. Here."

Something rattles down the air pipe, shoots out of it, and rolls across the floor like a marble and gets lost in the shadows.

"What was that?" Crystal says.

"Earl's glass eye."

"What? Jesus Christ!"

"Uh-oh. Lon's here. You want me to stay or leave?"

"Jesus Christ, Anita. What did you do to Earl? What's he—?"

Lon's voice comes through the air pipe: "I'm back from my open house."

"Anita threw . . . Anita, what—"

"What you say?" Lon says. He tries to open the hatch.

"Just go away. Both of you."

"I wanta talk," he says.

"I don't feel like it."

"I got time."

"I'm leaving," Anita says. "Don't you come out of there till you want to."

"Jesus, Anita. How did—"

"She's gone," Lon says. "You going to talk now?"

"Anita just threw a glass eye down here. I don't know where it's at, and I don't want to."

"What are you talking about?"

"Never mind. Now, go away."

"I want to know when the hell you're going to come out of there."

He sounds different, as though his voice were coming to her over a telephone. He has more of a hillbilly's twang and sounds more whiny than she's noticed before.

She paces the shelter, staying away from the corner where Earl's eye is. Lon is talking, but she's not listening. She circles the card table twice, stops at the air pipe.

She hears, "You'll catch your death of cold down there."

"It's just like my aunt June and Elvis."

"What is? Elvis who?"

"Elvis Presley."

"Your aunt June know Elvis Presley?"

"No. But you know how all those Elvis fanatics kept loving Elvis after he got fat? Well, Aunt June didn't. She told me she was just as big an Elvis fan as anybody, but when he started looking like a cow, she couldn't stand him anymore. She was embarrassed about ever liking him. She'd always had these erotic fantasies about him."

"She told you that?"

"She did. When I got older. Anyway, I loved Buck till he got his hand ripped off. Now I don't want that stump of his anywhere near me. I guess I'm a shallow person."

"Hell, no. It's understandable." Crystal stares at the candles. After a minute Lon says, "I was crazy for this girl in high school. Then she got her hair cut a new way, and she looked awful. I never talked to her again."

"That's terrible!"

"Well—"

"I mean, Buck didn't just get a haircut."

"Are you ever coming out of there?"

"I've got a lot of thinking to do yet."

"Aren't you bored? Can't you do your thinking up at the house? I got some pork chops in the freezer and some beer."

"You drink too much beer."

She walks away from the air pipe and can't hear what he's saying. She leans her forehead against the cold concrete wall and thinks of the night they met. Lon turned out to be the guy whose picture she'd seen every day of high school. He had been a baseball star. After he sat down at her table at the Kountry Klub and they had talked a little, she said, "Yeah, I know you. All through high school I walked into the lobby every day and saw your picture in the trophy case. You were like some . . . some immortal." He looked stunned. Anita said she had to go to the rest room and got up and never came back. Crystal went to find her. She finally looked outside and discovered Anita's GTO gone. For a minute she was in a panic, blowing puffs of breath through her chattering teeth into the cold air. Then Crystal felt relieved, as though a decision had been made for her. Back at their table, when the singer began a sweet ballad about how the loss of one love just made room for another, Crystal reached for Lon's hand.

A thought rushes into her head—if love is so damn special, why is it so easy to fall into? What made her love Lon or think she did? The line of his jaw, his long legs, his straight nose, his eyes? Lon's talk of some scheme involving a dozen farmettes worth sixty thousand dollars apiece? These all seem like bad reasons to love somebody, but she's not sure what the good reasons are. He seemed sweet. He wasn't missing any limbs. *Selfish tramp.* She wants to scream.

"Hey!" Lon bellows.

"Lon." She talks into the air pipe louder than she has been. "I don't want to be mean, but I've just got to decide if I should go back to Buck." She pauses. "You know, one night things almost worked out with him. He wrapped his stump up in all this gauze and stuffed a glove with toilet tissue so it'd seem he had a right hand."

"I don't wanta hear this."

"But then it fell off, and I screamed, and he looked so hurt, but I couldn't help it. Am I making any sense?" She pauses. "Do you know what I'm saying? I don't want to be mean to you or to him." She waits. "Lon? You there?"

*Selfish tramp.*

She drops down onto the cot, suddenly exhausted again.

# Twenty-six

Lon has been kneeling on the wet ground, talking and listening through a pipe sticking straight up a few feet from the bomb shelter's hatch. His pants are soaked through, and his knees ache from the cold. Standing, he brushes off his pants legs. Faintly Crystal's voice comes up from the ground, dissipates in the darkness. He doesn't want to hear about her husband.

He uses the rusty hatch to scrape mud off his shoes. He didn't know about the bomb shelter until several weeks after he moved onto the farm. He found it one morning when he went wandering through the high weeds behind the barn, trying to decide whether he really wanted to bother going into town to the real estate office. After looking around the shelter he stood at the card table and studied the photograph of the

farm family, and he imagined the stout wife frantically cranking the siren on the porch, the two little girls scurrying around
and grabbing their favorite dolls, the farmer running in from
the fields. He laughed at his vision. He laughed at the shelter.
He never imagined a woman of his would use it to hide from
him.

He walks to the house and takes a six-pack out of the refrigerator. He considers going back out and telling Crystal he
might have made a sale today but decides not to; anyway it's
best not to assume you have a sale until the commission check
is in your hands.

Women do like money, though. A TV commercial for a
jeweler in Cincinnati says, "Light her fire with diamonds."
Whenever he sees it, he tells himself he pities any poor rich
son of a bitch who has to give his woman a diamond to make
her hot. As he sits down in the living room with the six-pack
on his lap, he decides Crystal can rot in the bomb shelter for
all he cares.

She's pretty, like the weather girl on Channel 5, but the
prettier they are, the more they expect or the crazier they are.
Sometimes after sex he thinks he could maybe live without a
woman for the rest of his life, keep his life simple. But in a few
hours or days the mere memory of sex will not be enough.

Crystal likes drawn-out, slow sex and lots of orgasms, but
he'd just as soon do it fast, get it done, then snap his fingers
and make her disappear in a puff of smoke. Usually she starts
talking about how much she loves him, and he can't help
thinking she's a child and a fool.

"Do you love me?" she'll say.

"Yeah."

"Are you sure?"

"Yeah."

"I love *you*."

"I know."

"You're wonderful, Lon. Nobody's ever made me feel this way."

"What can I say? I'm a stud."

"Hey, you know what?"

"What?"

"I love you."

When she does that, he wants to break her neck. But he does care about her. She deserves to be treated well. He guesses he loves her, but he's loved lots of women, and love really doesn't mean that much, he's decided—doesn't mean he won't hurt her, doesn't mean he'll stay, doesn't mean she'll stay either.

The night he met her at the Kountry Klub, he wasn't looking for a woman. Some nights he did go there with women in mind. In the men's room, on the wall above a urinal, there was a poem he'd read every time he had to pee, and it would stick in his brain all night: "Fucked her standing, fucked her lying, smoked a joint, fucked her flying."

There were almost always a few people he'd gone to high school with at the Kountry Klub. Like Lon, some of them still wore their high school class rings. They always remembered him, but he would have sworn in court he'd never laid eyes on them. It amazed him how many guys his age were bald and had big guts; the ones he'd see at the Kountry Klub had all been married and divorced, some twice. Three years ago he ran into one woman he did remember, but just barely. In school she'd been a cute, quiet girl who made good grades and went out with only dorky guys who also made good grades. Over the years she'd put on fifty pounds and had been married and divorced three times. Lon went home with her, and she shouted a string of dirty words while he fucked her.

The night he met Crystal, he just wanted to get good and drunk. The loan application of a buyer had been rejected that afternoon. Day by day Lon was starting to realize he might not get rich being a real estate agent.

It was Saturday night, so the Kountry Klub was crowded. A group of women in tight jeans and cowboy hats were pretending, Lon suspected, that they were someplace interesting like Dallas, Texas, instead of Mount Orab, Ohio. They were dancing with each other and whooped like cowgirls on TV when they sighted a man they liked.

Lon was in a pretty good stupor, just studying the thickness of his beer mugs, when he heard close to his ear, "Excuse me." He turned his head, looked up, and saw an ugly woman a head taller than most of the men in the place. She leaned down so that her face was close to his. She had heavy purple lips. "My name's Anita, and I was wondering if you'd be interested in dancing?" Lon shuddered involuntarily, and she quickly said, "With my friend. She thinks you're nice-looking. I mean, good-looking but like a nice person too. She's too shy to ask you herself." Lon looked where Anita pointed and saw a pretty blonde wearing a little too much makeup. She was shaking her head and waving Anita back to their table. "She's been real depressed lately." Lon looked at Anita again. "I made her come out with me tonight. See, her husband's a farmer—"

"She's married?" Lon put his hands up in front of his chest, his palms forward as if to push Anita away.

"Well, yeah, but it's a dead marriage. He got his hand ripped off in a corn picker or something, and now she's just miserable. She doesn't want to be married to a one-handed man. Can you imagine ...?"

Lon looked across the room at the mechanical bull shoved in a corner with an OUT OF ORDER sign on it. Then he took another look at Crystal. Her eyes were wide, and her mouth was open, and she was gesturing at Anita, although Anita had her back to her. Two guys in International Harvester caps over at the bar were eyeing Crystal. Lon sat up. He had to admit she was a damn fine-looking girl. And he heard the men's room poem in his head.

# Twenty-seven

Live life one day at a time. He holds up a beer, toasting the blank TV screen, his tiny image reflected in it. One day at a time. One lay at a time. Yes. He drinks from the can, empties it, crushes it. One beer at a time.

He reaches over to the end table to check the answering machine, then picks up the telephone receiver to make sure it's working. Besides his Corvette, having two phones (this one and the one in the kitchen) is about as luxurious as his life gets.

After he replaces the receiver in the phone cradle, he accidentally knocks a vase of flowers off the table. He gets up to go to the kitchen for a towel so that he can wipe up the water, but he stops, looks around at all the flowers, then swings his arm at the vase on top of the TV.

He kicks over the ones on the dining-room floor.

In the kitchen he knocks flowers off the counters.

He lifts the vase from the top of the refrigerator, his chest heaving. He tells himself he has to stop. He looks at the flowers, smells them.

Then he flings the vase against the wall.

# Twenty-eight

Lloyd watches the redhead sit down and pick up a tattered magazine from the plastic chair beside her. He says, "Are you a waitress?"

She turns her head sharply and looks at him. Her blue eyes are really something. "What?"

He raises his voice above the noise of the machines. "You got white uniforms." He points at one of the washers she's using.

She looks down at the cover of her magazine, at Meryl Streep's picture. Then she looks at him again and sounds angry: "Maybe I'm a doctor."

"Well, in that case, I got this pain . . ." He leans forward on his chair and puts a hand on the small of his back.

"I work at Jackie's Café," she says flatly.

"I've eaten there. It's a good place. But my mashed potatoes were lumpy. You don't have anything to do with the mashed potatoes, do you?" He pauses, but she's opened the magazine. "You and me are both in the food-service industry. I'm the assistant manager of the McDonald's on River Avenue. Name's Mac. My friends call me Big."

She starts flipping the pages of the magazine fast. Lloyd doesn't know what's gotten into him. He used to act this way with girls in high school before he and Jenny started dating. His face feels hot. The big windows of the Laundromat are steaming up. He notices the woman has long red fingernails that match her bright lipstick, and he thinks of Freddy Krueger in *Nightmare on Elm Street*.

Lloyd stops his dryer, feels his clothes, and slips three more dimes into the machine. There's a crack of thunder outside, and the woman looks up and stares hard at the steamed-up window as if she could see through it. "This rain is really something," Lloyd says.

"It's never going to stop," she says.

He ambles over in her direction, but suddenly she softly hisses, "Shit!" and she jumps up and hurries to the pay phone by the Coke machine. He goes to the glass doors and wipes a circle to look through, but he turns so that he can watch the woman. She has her back to him, and her head is tucked down between her shoulders. He imagines his hands on her, his fingers kneading her nice bottom. It's been a long time since he had hold of a woman who would let him do as he pleased.

The redhead glances over her shoulder at him, then moves closer to the wall. With the washers and dryers going there's no way he can hear what she's saying.

He steps outside and stands in the rain. Cars swish by. He looks in the direction of the river, sees lights on in houses. If the night were clear, he would be able to see the outlines of mountains, black against a dark-blue sky.

He thinks he'll call Cole tomorrow. He can talk to Jenny's parents about Cole coming to live with him. Jenny's mom still calls Lloyd Larry. Jenny's old man doesn't call him anything. They know he has a good job now and bought a house. If he marries Donna, they'll have to give him Cole back without a fight. He'd like to get Donna to let her hair grow long again.

She told him today at work that at Wednesday meeting Brother Wallace said watching Smurf cartoons primed kids to become devil worshipers.

Deadpan, Lloyd said, "That's real scary."

"It *is!*" she said, her mouth stretching wide to show her messed-up teeth. "There's a lot more evil in this world than you've been exposed to."

He just glared at her. It occurs to him that if they had been characters on TV, she would have realized her mistake; she would have said, "Oh, I'm sorry. I wasn't thinking." But people on TV are better behaved than people in real life, he realizes. Evil—yeah, he knows something about evil. He wishes he could believe that Ted Bundy killed Jenny because Bundy's been executed, but in his nightmares about her murder the killer's face is always blurred or the killer is some actor Lloyd's seen in a movie.

A '73 Monte Carlo with mags goes by slow, and Lloyd remembers Jenny's smile. His gut suddenly feels hollowed out, and he wants to tell her everything is much better now. He owns a decent house, two blocks from an elementary school. No more houses on the river. No more hiding from the landlord or the repo guys from Best Buy Furniture. Then he smirks. "But my new washer broke," he says to the sky. He doesn't care that he's getting rained on. A passing car blares rock 'n' roll. In the pictures Jenny's parents send, Cole is looking more and more like Jenny. Lloyd looks toward the river again, sees tiny lights on the Kentucky side. "You're missing it," he says.

# Twenty-nine

While the redhead is folding her clothes, Lloyd decides to talk to her again. "You know, if you want, I'll follow you home and make sure you get there safe."

She doesn't look at him. He thinks, *You don't know a single thing about me.*

After she's gone, he reads some ads in a *Trading Post* newspaper and thinks about driving over to Mount Orab to see what's happening at the Kountry Klub. His eyes get heavy. His dryer shuts off, and the place is silent. He needs to see whether his clothes are dry, but he can't make himself move.

He dreams of being on the roof of the house he had on the riverbank. Donna and Cole are with him, and flood waters lift the house up gently and it floats down the river, barely swaying. The river is as blue as a stream in one of Cole's storybooks. Cole giggles. Donna smiles, and her teeth are straight.

Startled by a crack of thunder, Lloyd wakes up. He looks around, his eyes half hooded against the harsh light, uncertain about where he is. Then as his eyes adjust, he's startled by something else. In the corner of a bulletin board across the room, surrounded by fliers and scraps of paper, is half of Jenny's face, half of Jenny's smile, one of Jenny's eyes.

He looks away, out the window, which isn't steamed up anymore. The rain is falling in sheets, and the traffic has slowed down. He looks back at the bulletin board, then up at the ceiling, and closes his eyes. After a moment he brings his head down and pushes himself up, stands, blows air through his teeth. Crossing the room, he's light-headed.

It's a black-and-white flier, ten by thirteen, with "MISS-ING" in block letters at the top. This is the first one he's seen in more than a year. Lloyd and some friends and Jenny's parents put fliers up all over southern Ohio and northern Kentucky. For a few months he saw the picture everywhere he went. Before Lloyd let Jenny's parents take him, Cole would say, "Mommy!" when he saw one of the fliers. And Lloyd's heart would pause.

When the fliers began to get torn down, Lloyd was glad in a way because Jenny seemed to be waiting for him everywhere he went, torturing him with her eyes and her smile, never letting him escape the fact that she was the only woman he wanted and blaming him somehow for—for everything.

Covering Jenny is an advertisement for a flea market. A notice about free kittens. A baby-sitter's phone number. A scrap of paper about a reward for a lost dog.

Lloyd takes the thumbtacks out of the papers covering Jenny and moves them to another part of the board. The picture of Jenny is a blown-up version of the one in her high school yearbook. In the pupil of each of her eyes, there's a tiny light, a star. With the tip of a finger he touches her eyes. Then he takes the thumbtack out of the upper-right-hand corner of the flier, holds it in the air a moment, then puts it back. He looks at her smile, thinks of Donna.

He steps away from the bulletin board and looks around the Laundromat. A glare comes off the red and yellow and green plastic chairs. Outside, the rain pours.

When he turns back to Jenny, he hears the memory of music. He squeezes his eyes shut. In the center of the darkness Jenny appears in a frilly blue dress, sitting on a white porch swing. The music twangs, and her eyes express her loneliness, the loneliness of the dead.

# Thirty

Pamela still has nightmares about finding Bobby dead: she shivers in her dream from the iciness of the trailer; a can of gun cleaner, Hoppe's number 9, sat on the beat-up coffee table in front of the sofa; the colors of everything were unnaturally bright, like on "Miami Vice," which she used to kind of like because of Don Johnson, but the show got old, and Don Johnson has become just another man who couldn't hold her interest.

The only difference between her nightmare and what really happened is that in the dream Matt is there, on the floor, a baby crawling around in a diaper, slapping at the pool of blood by Bobby's head and looking at Pamela and giggling.

"Jesus, you're sweatin' like a pig," Lloyd says, and puts his hand on her shoulder.

Pamela is sitting up in bed, her heart pounding. She tilts her head to look at Lloyd and tries to remember why he's here. The straps of her nightgown have slipped off her shoulders, and Lloyd is staring at the tops of her breasts. "You saying I'm fat?" she says.

"Naw. You have a bad dream?"

"Yeah."

"What was it about?"

"Nothing. I forget." The room is full of the grayness of early morning.

Lloyd doesn't say anything for a minute. Then he says, "You got a lot of moles."

"Yeah, I guess."

"I knew a girl in school had a mole on her neck that turned green. She found out it was cancer."

Pamela sees herself in the dresser mirror across from the bed; her shoulders are rounded, fat-looking; there are dark crescents under her eyes. Lloyd leans his head against hers and looks into the mirror too. "What you seein', Pam?"

He's twenty-one, he told her. He looks incredibly young, like all those guys in the singing group Matt likes so much, New Kids on the Block.

He puts his hand under the sheet, and she feels it on her thigh. She doesn't have any panties on.

"You know I'm thirty," she says.

"You told me that last night."

His hand moves up her thigh, and she says, "I've got to go to work, Lloyd." She gets off the bed and reaches for her robe lying across the back of a chair she got for three dollars at a garage sale. "It was nice meeting you. I mean, like I said last night, I remember when you used to sing at the Kountry Klub, but I never met you."

"You got to work on Sunday?"

"Sure do."

"But it's not even five o'clock, for Christ's sake."

"Yeah, I know."

She flicks on the ceiling light as she leaves the room, gets a towel from the hall closet, and goes into the bathroom. She locks the door.

She stays in the shower until the water turns cold. Then she dries her hair until the blow dryer starts smoking. She slaps at the air and decides to trim her toenails. She listens for the sound of the front door closing.

Finally she leaves the bathroom. Lloyd's clothes are still on the bedroom floor, and she softly hisses, "Shit!" She finds him in Matt's room on his knees in his jockey shorts, pushing one of Matt's toy trucks across the floor and making a rumbling sound in his throat.

"You got a kid, don't ya?" he says, and stands up, holding the toy and spinning its wheels.

"Yeah."

"Where is he?"

"He's at my mom's."

"Why?"

Pamela sighs. "Because he likes her and she likes him."

"Does he ever see his dad?" Lloyd sets down the truck and picks up a toy soldier holding a long rifle.

"His dad's dead."

"I thought you said last night you was divorced."

"I'm divorced from my first husband. My second husband shot himself . . . accidentally. It was before my little boy was born. I didn't even know I was pregnant at the time."

Lloyd gapes at her and says, "Boy, you been around."

"I'm sorry."

"No. I got a boy. He's—"

"Listen, Lloyd. I really do have to get to work."

"Okay. You go save lives. You want me to stay here and wait for you to come home?"

"No, you go on."

He grins. "Maybe I'll catch the early service at the Holy Roller church."

"Okay." She looks around but has no idea what she's looking for. She wonders what horrors Matt's hidden under his bed.

"Don't you think I'm funny?" Lloyd asks.

"What?"

"I was jokin'."

"Okay."

Pamela goes to her bedroom and gets a uniform out of her closet and takes it into the bathroom to put it on. When she comes out, Lloyd is dressed. He has on blue jeans and a Western shirt and cowboy boots. At least he doesn't wear a cowboy hat. After all, this is Ohio, and a cowboy hat would make him look like a complete fool.

She grabs her purse and mumbles that she's really late now.

Lloyd follows her to the front door, saying, "It's been real nice, Pam."

"It was nice meeting you, too, Lloyd."

"I like the way you make a lot of noise."

She digs her car keys out of her purse, holds the front door open for him, then pulls the door shut and makes sure it's locked.

His car, a rusty Camaro with bald tires, blocks her Chevette.

Everything is covered with ice. She gets her plastic window scraper out of her car. Lloyd takes it from her and starts chipping away at the ice on her windshield. "Whoever built your carport didn't know what he was doin'." Lloyd points at the leaning carport, then goes back to working on the ice. "Thing's gonna fall over one of these days. They must not of used enough cement around the supports. See those cracks?"

Pamela doesn't look at the carport. "That's good enough. You don't need to do any more. Just as long as I have a little hole to look through." She opens her car door, tosses her purse onto the passenger seat, and gets in.

"I'd sue him if I was you. My uncle used to work construction, and I know something about it."

She closes her door, rolls down the window, and says, "I'm real late, Lloyd."

"Oh, sure. Well, Pam, you'll be hearin' from me, don't worry." He leans down to her window, and his puckered lips come at her. She kisses him quickly and starts the car.

"Pam."

"What?" She squints her eyes at the odometer as if she were trying to figure something out.

"Here's your scraper."

"Thanks."

"One more thing."

"What?"

"I don't know you real good, but I know what kind of person you are, and I think I could love you."

Pamela nods twice and puts the car in gear.

Lloyd jumps back. "Hold on. Let me get my beast out of your way."

He backs his car out and waits for her to pull out. She's afraid to look around at the other houses. She's afraid she'll see one or more of her neighbors eyeballing this scene.

He follows her until she's almost to the county hospital in West Union. Every time she looks in the rearview mirror, he's riding her bumper and grinning at her. She never stops amazing herself. Here she is pretending she has to go to work to get away from a guy she threw herself at six hours ago.

He toots his horn twice before turning onto Highway 40 that goes to Portsmouth. He waves, but Pamela doesn't wave back.

Pamela drives past the hospital. She misses Matt, thinks about going over to her mother's and getting him, but she doesn't want to have to explain why she's wearing a uniform on her day off, and if she gets him this early, she'll be worn to a frazzle and screaming at him by evening.

A light sleet is falling. It was sleeting the morning two months ago when Roy brought the lumber for the carport, the morning Pamela made up her mind not to marry him.

She had woken up feeling good, although the house was cold and the wind howled outside. Often Matt got in bed with her in the middle of the night and never failed to pee all over her sheets, but he had stayed in his room for once and was still asleep.

Pamela moved around quietly, then shut Matt's door so that she could run the electric mixer. Roy was coming over for breakfast at nine.

The oven warmed the kitchen. The whir of the mixer struck Pamela as a sound of celebration. She was making Roy cinnamon-swirl muffins. As she was spooning the mix into the muffin pan, she heard *girl*. Not Bobby's voice but Roy's. A word left over from the night before. It had risen to the ceiling, floated there all night. *Girl. Perfect. Beautiful. Love.* The words drifted in Pamela's head like snowflakes.

She set the timer on top of the stove. When she opened

the oven, a foul smell escaped, the remnants of old black food burning again.

Pamela heard Roy's Grand Prix in the driveway. She leaned across the sink to see out the window, to the side of the house. She blinked several times. Lumber stuck out the back window of the car.

She rushed outside in her robe to get a better look at what he'd done to his car. She stood on her narrow, cracked walk gaping. Pieces of glass lay on the space behind the backseat. A few shards remained in the corners of the window.

"What did you do?"

"Girl, it's freezing out here." He wrapped himself around her. She felt smothered by his big coat and beard. "I got down to the lumberyard soon as they opened this mornin' and realized there was no way I could haul the beams I needed in my trunk, and God only knew when they'd deliver the load. Christmas is . . ." He tried to pull her toward the house, but she resisted.

Pamela twisted away and looked again at the lumber. The boards started on the passenger side of the dashboard, butting up against the windshield, and extended out through where the back window used to be. A small sticker on one of the pieces of lumber said "solid oak."

She looked at her Chevette parked in front of Roy's car. It was six years old and a little beat-up, but at least she hadn't been fool enough to smash out the rear window so she could haul lumber. Her anger swelled. The waste. Stupid. Lon never . . . Not even Bobby would have done something this crazy. Mingled with her anger like a thin swirl of cinnamon in her muffins was the understanding that Roy did this for her. He did this because he was so eager to please, so frantic to get the gift built by Christmas.

He grabbed her again and pulled her into his chest, smothered her. "Let's get inside, baby."

Stupid. Crazy. She pushed out of his arms. Sharp needles of freezing rain stung her as she gaped again at the car, waiting to understand why the smashed window was so important. Why didn't she laugh? Should she thank him?

"You're gonna catch your death from cold, girl."

She hugged herself. Then she felt a subtle smile bloom as she realized that this was the excuse she'd been waiting for.

# Thirty-one

**R**oy didn't finish the carport until the middle of January. He got it half done and had to tear it down and start over because he discovered he'd done something all wrong. He persisted although Pamela had told him she was certain she could never marry him. She told him she didn't love him. Forget the carport, she said. Forget it, please. But he kept at it, hanging around the house nearly every evening, playing with Matt, showing him how to use tools. Pamela fixed him snacks when he took breaks. She even kept having sex with him until the carport was finished. It was like having a debt she was still making payments on.

But she never let Roy stay all night. Never. Not once. Not even before Christmas when she was on the verge of giving in to his proposal of marriage, on the verge of shoving out of her head all the fears and inhibitions that came from having had two bad marriages.

She has worried a lot lately about her coldness, a coldness that won't let her get emotionally close to a man, won't let her do things like have a man stay all night. Last night with Lloyd was a test she gave herself. She picked up a stranger at the Kountry Klub and brought him home, and after he made fast, clumsy love to her, she said, "You'll sleep here, won't you?" She was determined to prove to herself she was normal.

Now she guesses she failed the test. She remembers taking a history exam in ninth grade: she would have passed, but she forgot to put her name on the test. Maybe the test she gave herself last night was stupid, she thinks as she drives out into the countryside. She must have been crazy. She was somebody else last night. Boy, was she "easy." Lloyd didn't even have to sing for her.

She has turned down a gravel road and isn't thinking about where she's going when she passes the farm that Lon grew up on. The fields are full of weeds, and about fifty motorcycles are parked around the house and barn. A motorcycle gang owns the place now. Pit bulls are chained to the trees. Pamela thinks about what sweet people Lon's parents were.

She turns around in a farmer's driveway to go back to town. When she passes Lon's old place again, she suddenly realizes that Lloyd reminded her of Lon. She didn't know what it was last night, but she certainly did like something about Lloyd. He was tall and lean and wore a boyish grin. His dark eyes were nice, and she liked his tight blue jeans and the way he moved as they danced.

Lon.

Back in West Union she passes Jack's Eats and the courthouse. She looks at the cloudy, empty windows of William's

Hardware and Be Beautiful Beauty Salon. It's been years since those two places went out of business. At the corner of Main, past the barbershop, West Union Drugs has been turned into West Union Video Rentals. She turns down Dogwood Street and passes Valley Realty. She's heard Lon's a real estate agent now, and she wonders how he's doing. It's hard to believe he's doing something like that, but maybe there are things about him she never knew, or maybe he's just grown up.

She feels she should be doing something constructive, so she turns back onto Main, then into the parking lot of the Kroger supermarket, making a grocery list in her head. But then she notices the store's not open yet.

Heading home, she starts worrying about what Lloyd might do. She knows a nurse at the hospital who had a guy sleep outside her apartment door every night for a week. Pamela hears all the time on TV and the radio about women getting murdered by guys obsessed with them. In high school, when she was a thin cheerleader, there were nerdy guys who would keep calling her and sending her flowers and writing her love letters, hoping she'd agree to go out with them. Her friend Wanda called them "horny rejects." It was all a joke. The guys were jokes. But now Pamela knows that the horny rejects commit a lot of the murders she hears about.

Pamela thinks hard about all of Lloyd's expressions and the things he talked about, searching for hints of a psychopathic mind. Then she thinks of Bobby, his skinny arms, his mop of hair, his hands shoved into the pockets of his blue jeans—*You don't love me no more, do you?* She thinks of Lon, has an image of him stroking a baseball cleanly into the out-field for a base hit. Then she remembers a nurse who ran away with a doctor a couple of years ago. She abandoned her husband and three little girls because she thought the doctor was a combination of Tom Cruise and Jesus Christ. They moved to Missouri, and in a year the doctor left her for a respiratory therapist.

Maybe, Pamela hopes, Lloyd will write her off as a one-night stand to brag to his buddies about. He's probably got girlfriends his own age anyway. Roy did all right. After he finished the carport last month, he stopped coming around, which really surprised her. In two weeks he was engaged to a hairstylist in Portsmouth with four kids. He came by her house to tell her about it—not to be nasty, just to let her know he was all right, was happy. The next day she saw his fiancée's engagement picture in the paper. The woman had kind of a skinny, pretty face but a stupid puffed-up hairdo.

Yeah, men bounce back quick. They can switch to a new woman the way they switch channels on TV.

She let Roy into her life just so far, and yes, she was the one who did the rejecting, the one who didn't want to get married, but still, his finding someone else so lightning-quick gnaws at her heart.

But Lon—Lon has never remarried. Suddenly Pamela thinks she'd like to see Lon.

She's been mean to Lon over the past six years since he came back to Adams County, snubbing him whenever they've run into each other. There's no reason, though, why they can't be friendly, can't keep up with what's going on in each other's life. It's only natural for them to be curious about each other. The last time she saw him, he was wearing that old green suit of his. Pamela laughed about it with her mother. "Yes, I've seen him in it," her mother said, shaking her head and frowning.

"For God's sake, we got married in that suit," Pamela said. "I mean, he did."

She makes a plan: Today or tomorrow she'll drop by the real estate office. For a short visit. Just to say hi. She'll wear her black dress, which makes her look thinner. She'll extend her hand and shake, tell him she just wanted to see how he was. She'll tell him he looks good. If they talk awhile and if no other people are around, she will say she has no ill will about the past. It was all long ago, and they were kids. Some things don't work out. Because of circumstances at the time.

It will be good for her, she thinks, to clear the air between her and Lon after twelve years. Of course she won't do anything foolish. She certainly won't tell him about Lloyd, about sleeping with a kid who reminded her of him.

And she won't go out with Lon—assuming he would want to date a tub like her.

## Thirty-two

When Crystal wakes up, the candles have burned out. She can't see a thing. But out of nowhere she has a revelation: The bomb shelter isn't safe at all; if air—and even glass eyes—can come down that pipe, then so can nuclear radiation and a million other things. The shelter is no escape from the end of the world. It's only a temporary hiding place.

She feels around, puts her hand in a pool of warm candle wax, then finds the ladder to get out of the shelter. It's a dark night, no stars, no moon. She hurries through the wet weeds and puddles to the house, freezing.

There's a pile of beer cans on the floor in front of the sofa, and the TV is going, and smashed vases and flowers are strewn everywhere. She feels assured that getting hooked up with Lon was just a big mistake; she wants nothing to do with a man who slaps her and smashes vases.

She takes a quick shower, blow-dries her hair, and puts on makeup. If Lon walks in, she'll tell him the truth: Buck is her husband, and he's been good to her, and he's had a horrible thing happen and received no comfort from her. She is now, finally, before it's too late, going to do the right thing.

The bathroom is warm and steamy, and she's overcome by her power to make people happy. She'll make her parents happy and Buck happy. Buck's life will start anew. Crystal gazes at herself in the mirror, acknowledges that she's beautiful.

# Thirty-three

Lon accelerates although he's approaching a curve, and the two six-packs of beer on the passenger seat slide a couple of inches. It's past five in the morning. He was the last customer to leave the Kountry Klub. Even then he got in his Corvette but didn't want to leave. He decided to wait for a new waitress whose name he didn't know. She had a fat, flat nose and a big ass; he thought she'd be easy, but when she came out of the club and Lon was there in the lot following her to her car, saying he really admired the way she carried a tray, she pulled a cannister of Mace out of her purse.

He had to settle for stopping at a Quick Stop for the six-packs and some licorice sticks.

The Corvette's headlights catch the sign that says ENTER-ING ADAMS COUNTY.

Lon read recently that Corvettes have the highest death rate of any car in America, but he finds it hard to believe, the way its wide tires hug the road and its long, graceful front end keeps things at a distance. The Vette is a hard, silky cock. A Yugo, a Dodge K-car, Escorts—those strike him as limp dicks, death traps.

His tie pinches, and he loosens it. Fuck if he's going to drive a Volvo. Until a year ago he had worn a tie no more than a half dozen times in his life. Now he wears almost nothing but his suit. He thinks people are nicer to him because of it.

He takes the long way to his farm so that he can pass through West Union. He cruises up the street Pamela's mother lives on. He remembers her living room was small, the carpet worn out. What he remembers best is the way the place always smelled like stale cookies for some reason. Lights are on in the house; Darrell's old car is in the driveway. Lon hopes that when he gets home, there'll be a message on the answering machine. He'll have to phone Darrell in the morning and apologize for not being in. Of course he won't say he was out getting beer. He remembers Darrell's warning not to drink and drive.

He shakes his head, thinking about Darrell being a county deputy and having a wife. When Lon was married to Pamela, Darrell was only thirteen, a pudgy little kid with freckles who called Lon Bro. Darrell introduced Lon to his friends as his brother, not his brother-in-law. Once, Darrell asked him to beat up a kid: "He grabbed my Mike Schmidt card and ripped it in half, just to be a turd. Kid's name is Roger, and I can tell you where he lives, and I want you to beat the shit out of him. Okay, Bro?"

Lon said, "What you think I am? The West Union Mafia?"

This afternoon, when Darrell recited the phone number where he could be reached, Lon immediately recognized it, had never forgotten it: Pamela's number, a number Lon called hundreds of times when he was in high school. He used to make a list of topics to talk with her about because he was afraid that he would run out of things to say and that she would think he was boring.

# Thirty-four

Crystal's car is gone. He parks his Corvette in the barn and closes the huge doors and walks to the house. The wind blows his suit coat open, blows his tie over his shoulder. He has a six-pack in each hand, gripping them hard, as if he might drop them.

On the porch he pauses, turns around, and looks at the hulking barn, black against the black sky, and thinks about bikers living on his parents' farm. And about Pamela's dead husband. Lon pictures the scrawny son of a bitch rotting in the ground, taking the image from an old horror movie Yvonne Strickland was in. He sees his mama throwing corn kernels to chickens. He's making himself think of these things because for the moment anything is better than thinking of Crystal. These other things are farther away, more easily dealt with. So he sees his daddy hunched over a glass of whiskey. He sees Pamela's new, thick face.

But then he sees Crystal slowly unbuttoning her blouse, her lips parted, her head thrown back so that her long neck is stretched—exposed and vulnerable. He thinks of vampire butterflies.

He looks at the crank siren. Banshee. He looks up into the black sky, searching for the moon that he knows has to be hiding somewhere.

# Thirty-five

**B**uck has left the porch light on—for her, Crystal is certain. The door is unlocked.

Yes, this is home, she thinks as she walks through the house. Taking up an entire wall in the living room are framed pictures of herself—in an Easter dress, in her Miss Pumpkin Festival dress, in her Miss Adams County dress, in her prom dress, in her graduation gown, in her wedding dress (she's turned sideways so her cast is hidden). The house is still full of her smells, her powders and perfumes and air fresheners. And Buck's clean, simple masculine scent. This is where she belongs. She picks up an antique cut-glass vase her grandmother gave her.

In the bedroom she finds Buck asleep. His hair is tousled, and his mouth is open a little. She thinks of how white and straight his teeth are. He needs a shave, which makes him look rugged.

But when she leans over him, reaching her fingers toward his face to awaken him with a gentle touch, with her love, she's startled to see that down at his side his stump isn't wrapped up. The end of it is puckered like the ends of a tube of sausage. It's dark purple, the color fading to his elbow.

She takes a step back from the bed, looks down the hall, and sees the sofa in the living room. She thinks how it should be moved to a spot closer to the fireplace.

Then she imagines she turns and leans over to kiss Buck's cheek.

She imagines sitting down on the edge of the bed as he opens his eyes, blinking against the light; and she takes his big hand with its thick fingers, the nails long and ragged, and she says, *I'm back.*

But instead of stepping toward him, she steps toward the doorway and touches a strip of molding, sliding her finger along a groove. She moves her lips, trying to practice the words *I'm back.*

# About the Author

**Mark Spencer** grew up on a farm in southern Ohio and now lives in Lawton, Oklahoma, and teaches creative writing at Cameron University. His fiction has appeared in a variety of magazines including *The Laurel Review*, *Short Story*, *South Dakota Review*, *Florida Review*, *The Chariton Review*, and *Beloit Fiction Journal*. His collection of short stories *Spying on Lovers* won the Patrick T. T. Bradshaw Book Award. He is also the author of a collection entitled *Wedlock*.